MORE
TALES
OF
MYSTERY AND
SUSPENSE

RUSS CROSSLEY

53RD STREET PUBLISHING

More Tales of Mystery and Suspense

Russ Crossley

Published by 53rd Street Publishing

Publishing

trade paperback ISBN 978-1-927621-35-6
Ebook ISBN 978-1-927621-09-7

Also available in E-book

53rd Street Publishing
www.53rdstreetpublising.com

Table of Contents

Introduction

I have been a fan of the mystery since I first read The Hardy Boys mysteries when I was a boy. I remember reading Mary Robert Reinhart's, The Bat which chilled and thrilled me. If you can find a copy I highly recommend it. Of course I, like many mystery fans, read the Adventures of Sherlock Holmes. He wasn't the first private detective, but certainly the most famous, especially since the character has been probably the most depicted in film and television, and is still a favorite today. I have seen so many hours of film and television mystery I can recite the retread plots for you (but I won't).

Some stories stand out in my memory more than others. I would not want to live in Cabot Cove, Maine nor be a friend or relation of Mrs. Fletcher, but I love the mysteries both on television and in the books. And Mr. Monk's unorthodox style resonates with me, again in both mediums. Nor would I wish to live In Midsomer in England. The 1975 Ellery Queen series with the late Jim Hutton in the lead role is still a particular favorite of mine of the amateur detective subgenre. All these mysteries regardless of style have one thing in common, the hero seeks to make the world right again. And the usually succeed.

In this collection I have put together five stories encompassing the type of mystery and crime fiction I enjoy. Detectives, both private and police, solving crimes. Love, corruption, and greed abound in mystery fiction. I have included stories that demonstrate how these volatile aspects of the human psyche fight to make us stray onto the dark side of our nature and too often bring out the worst aspects of otherwise good people. I assure you justice will prevail, one way or another.

I hope you enjoy these stories as much as I did writing them.

Russ Crossley
Vancouver, Canada
March 2012

Skullduggery

I PARKED NEXT TO a late model green pickup that was beside a cherry red Taurus in front of the bar off the main building of the Skull Inn. After turning off the cars engine I sat in silence wondering why I agreed to leave the city. I hate the country. But a guys gotta make a living. Especially a guy like me.

The inn's owner, Bum Walker, invited me here saying he had a job for me. He told me Big Pete Scarpella, from the old Jersey neighborhood where I grew up, recommended me. Pete and a few select others of my contemporaries from the old days, are people I still stay in touch with. I'd been in Boston two months ago visiting a friend when I was first introduced to Bum.

Skullduggery

I've been hiding in plain sight under an assumed name for the past two years since I'd been in the unenviable position of meting out justice for the murder of Sunshine Robespierre. My nom de plume these days is Allan Harper, at least that's what my counterfeit id papers say. In my old life I used to be Jazz Stiletto, PI, shamus, dick, gumshoe, or just plain old private investigator if you prefer. My PI license ended after the Sunshine case, after which I hit the road with not much more than the clothes on my back. I've never been a nester, roaming is in my nature, but I really enjoyed the PI business, seediness and all. This man for hire life didn't fit me well. I just wasn't comfortable and wore my new life as it were an ill fitting suit.

I ran my tongue over my dry lips. I was beginning to regret my decision to quit smoking this particular week. Maybe a steady stream of coffin nails weren't so bad after all, there must be worse things, right?. It had been raining all day and now the rain hit the roof harder reminding me that into every life a little rain must fall, but why did have to be mine. I wish I chewed gum. My insurance, in case anyone recognized me, was the 380 Smith and Wesson I kept hidden in the small of my back beneath my jacket. Without a weapon I may as well be naked, and I wasn't going into uncharted territory without insurance.

I turned off the engine of the rented Hyundai Elantra and sat in silence surveying the gathering gloom around me listening to shrill cries of crows, their harsh voices cutting through the now pounding rain. It sounded like the murder of crows calling to each other from the maple, oak and hemlock trees surrounding the parking lot knew something I didn't. Crows have an instinct for trouble, or so I'm told.

The Skull Inn is located on the southern tip of Massachusetts not far from Gloucester situated on a cliff overlooking the ocean. According to my research the Skull Inn is named after the ship of a notorious local pirate that broke up on the rocks at the base of the cliff in 1789.

The sign over the door to the bar read Skullduggery. The name didn't bode well for my involvement with the owner. Before I agreed to the meeting I did some research on him as well.

Bum (birth name Walter) Walker arrived in Boston from Florida in 1995 where he bought an Irish bar. He's 47 years old, unmarried, loved playing the ponies, and from what my sources tell me made a very good living in Boston. He sold his bouncing baby bar in 2009 then moved here after purchasing this establishment.

Skullduggery

From the condition of the rough wood siding covered in green moss and the chipped paint on the wood framed windows it didn't appear the Skull Inn was as successful as the Boston watering hole had been.

I got out of the car and immediately my mouth and nose were filled with the smells of damp turning leaves, musty moss, with an undercurrent of salt briny air. In the distance was the faint roar of ocean waves pounding against the jagged rocks where the Inn's namesake had ended its illustrious career of skullduggery over two hundred years ago.

My runners crunched on the gravel as I made my way to the entrance to the bar. I've always loved a good bar. The hinges on the door squealed as I pulled it open and went inside.

The smells of stale tobacco whiskey and beer sending a familiar warmth into my belly and a sense of nostalgia over me. For me every bar is a little piece of heaven on Earth. The door squeaked on its hinges as it closed then slammed shut behind me.

Across the room, running along one wall for the length of the room, stood a gleaming oak bar. A real beaut. Behind the bar stood a man with a bulbous nose and dark, beady eyes.

The wall behind him comprised of a dimly lighted, wall length mirror interrupted by glass shelves filled with a wide variety of liquors in a rainbow of colors.

The worn brown carpet on the floor muffled my footsteps. One end of the room opened onto the connecting hallway to the Inn's lobby.

I approached the bar and climbed onto one of the tall padded wooden bar stools sitting in front of the bar.. The bartender offered me a tight smile then began to wipe the bars shiny surface with a white rag. At one of the bar, about ten feet away, sat a lone woman who appeared to be the high side of forty with well tended dyed blonde hair, smoking a cigarette with a glass of white wine in front of her. Her gray-green eyes regarded me dispassionately.

Her companion — he sat two stools away from the woman so I use the term loosely — wore a tweed sport coat with a sky blue tie over a white shirt. He appeared to be about fifty and his eyes flitted away from mine when I looked in his direction. A bottle of beer sat in front of him.

The bartender stopped his wiping and dropped the rag in the sink to his right. "What can I get ya?" he said to me.

"Soda water, thanks. You Walker?" The man matched Big Pete's physical description of Walker, broad shoulders, a barrel chest, and thick arms

The bartender had been cool up to this point, but when I mentioned the name of the owner he hesitated and his eyes narrowed. He peered at me with one eyebrow arched.

"You a cop?" he asked.

Interesting reaction. A man who enters a bar dressed in blue jeans, a black tee shirt under a dark red windbreaker, hardly looks like a cop. If I'd been in my old PI get up, Wal-mart suit with matching leather shoes, badly in need of polishing, I would have expected such a reaction. I shook my head. "No. Why? You need one?"

The bartender guffawed and slapped the bar with the palm of one meaty hand. "Good one. You must be Harper." He stuck out one hand which I shook.

His handshake was firm displaying confidence. I often assessed the handshake of a potential client before I accepted a job. A limp handshake made me hesitate. In this case the usual tells were moot since I'd already accepted the job whatever it might be.

When I spoke with Big Pete he confirmed Walker was okay and the job legit, but he didn't want to tell me anything about it.

He said I should hear Walker out, then decide where to go from there. All very mysterious, but a guy needs to eat and Walker said he'd pay me five hundred a day plus expenses.

"Let me get your soda then we'll go to my office where we can talk in private." He turned away to get a glass.

I glanced at the two at the end of the bar. The woman didn't appear to be listening, her attention fixed on the mirror across the back wall. The man appeared to be as nervous as a mouse, his hands clasping and unclasping the beer bottle, his eyes staring down at the bar, looking everywhere except at the woman. Beads of sweat dotted his forehead yet the room temperature was a little on the cool side.

I smiled wanly as Walker handed me the glass then motioned for me to follow him. He walked to a counter door at the end of the bar which he swung upward stepped through, dropped then led the way toward the lobby. We crossed the lobby, there was no one at the front desk, to a door marked Private.

Walker stopped and pulled a keychain from his pocket. The fob on the keychain was a rabbits foot. I smirked inwardly. Guy must believe in luck. Not me. I'm more of things-happen-for-a-reason kinda guy.

Before I was forced out of the cops I closed a lot of cases by following the evidence. I never once solved a crime because I got lucky. There was always a good reason. Not always a neat-as-a-bow reason, or even one that I understood, but always a reason.

I followed Walker into the office. The room was cramped with a cheap desk and single chair near the back wall, and an old dark green file cabinet to the left of the desk. The walls were unadorned and the desk was covered in stacks of disorganized papers some of which appeared to be bills. Two newspapers sections were scattered across the top of the mess. An older model computer monitor sat on one corner of the desk.

Walker moved around behind the desk and sat in the worn leather chair causing it to squeak. I sat in a worn wooden captains chair across from him. I wanted to set my glass down but didn't want to leave any rings on the papers on the desk so I cradled it in my hand.

Walker leaned back in his chair regarding me with his beady eyes. I'd seen such intimidation tactics in the past so needless to say I was amused. I raised the glass to my lips and took a small sip.

He broke our mutual silence first. Round one, Jazz. "Big Pete tells me you used to be a PI and a cop. That true?" I nodded. "Good. I have a big problem and I need someone like you to take care of it."

"What's the problem? " I asked casually.

"I host a murder mystery game at the Inn every weekend. Ya know, everyone is assigned a role, victim, killer, suspects, and detectives.... The heroes, suspects, and villains keep their identity secret while the participants ask questions of each other until the killer is discovered. I provide the Inn's facilities and provide a meal. It's all in good fun, and adds to my bottom-line."

"You need me for a game?"

Walker grunted, one corner of his mouth curled up slightly and his eyes crinkled at the corners. "No. Of course not." The corners of eyes drooped and became hard as steel as the smile faded from his lips. "Someone attending the game this weekend is going to murder me."

***

I sat at the bar sipping from a large glass of soda water with a slice of lime floating in the bubbles. On the bar stool next to me sat Simon Pedlar, the fellow with the nervous disposition who Bum (yeah, he told me to call him Bum) introduced me to when we returned to the bar from his office.

After Bum dropped his nuke on me about the threat to his life anyone I met from this point forward was a potential murder suspect.

Skullduggery

Naturally I acted as friendly as possible, at least as friendly as possible for me, a natural loner with a surly manner. Working and playing well with others is not one of my gifts.

Pedlar is Bum's accountant and had been since he purchased the inn in '09. He made his office in the nearby village of Lead, a small town about five miles away I'd passed through on my way here. Bum assured me Pedlar's nervousness had nothing to do with the information he'd provided, his nervous condition was more hereditary than anything else. Not that I doubted Bum, but from my perspective no one was off the hook as potential killer.

Pedlar, as keeper of the books, knew more about the financial condition of the Inn and Bum than anyone else. I'd seen too many people murdered where money was the primary motive, more than any other reason, and if the sum was large enough even possibly multiple murder victims.

One thing for sure this sweaty, nervous mouse didn't look like a man who could kill anybody, especially a robust character such as Bum Walker. He hadn't kept in perfect physical shape but he easily outweighed the accountant by sixty or seventy pounds.

For a man on the low side of fifty, Bum Walker appeared to be the man you'd expect for a former Miami street kid who spent his youth in bar fights.

"So, Mr. Pedlar, you here for the weekends festivities?" I said to my stool mate.

The corners of Pedlar's mouth curled up slightly. "Ya, I often come to Bum's murder mystery weekends. I love a good mystery. I read a lot," he nodded as he explained.

"How long you been his accountant?" I asked changing the subject.

Pedlar eyed me with one eyebrow arched. "You IRS?"

Why did everyone I'd met seem to think I'm in law enforcement? Had someone taped a sign on my back I didn't know about? "No. I'm a consultant. Security." Since I left my PI life I've used the old nebulous consultant label scam favored by disgraced bankers. I added security this time because I enjoyed making this guy nervous. He was beginning to get on my nerves in his sweat stained suit and too thin tie.

Pedlar nodded. He took a sip from his beer then said, "Bum and I go way back. I used to work for him in Boston."

I nodded and turned my attention to gazing into the mirror on the wall.

I focused on Maggie Townsend seated two stools away from us. Bum told me Maggie's, fifty-three, a widow who lives alone surviving on her late hubby's life insurance. She has two grown children who ignore her from opposite ends of the continent.

But I was distracted by my mental notebook which was in full rewind mode. If Pedlar knew Bum in Boston then Bum Walker lied to me. He said Pedlar started working for him in '09. I really hate it when clients lie to me. Even small lies, as was most likely the case with this one.

I watched as Maggie got off the stool wobbled off toward the washrooms at the other end of the room.

"You here for the game?" I said turning my attention back to the accountant.

"Yeah. It relaxes me."

I stifled a laugh. I couldn't imagine anything relaxing this guy. "You play the villain or a good guy?"

Pedlar grinned. "Neither. I always play a guest. I've never solved one of these things yet, but it's fun."

"Uh, uh. So what kind of shape are Bum's books in?" I peered into the mirror watching Pedlar for his reaction.

The easy slightly drunken grin disappeared from his lips and his cheeks drained of color.

His lean frame visibly stiffened his hands began to tremble. He stopping the shaking by tightening his grip on the beer bottle with one hand while hiding the other by dropping it out of sight below the edge of the bar. There's always a great deal of satisfaction in shaking up someone's world.

"Bad shape are they?" I added. I took a sip from my glass. The soda cooled my tongue.

His brow furrowed. "I didn't say that." His sharp tone of voice cut me like a knife.

Shaken and now stirred him, and I was just warming up. I raised both hands in mock surrender as I rose from the stool. "Sorry. I didn't mean anything by it."

I watched his eyes glare at me as I walked behind, then past him to the other side of Maggie's stool just in time for her to exit the ladies room and start making her way back across the bar. Her red rimmed eyes were locked on her destination, the stool next to where I'd moved.

I watched her coming, her legs trembling from the struggle to stay vertical. I knew she'd make it probably for a few hours yet, if she slowed down her intake of booze. I'd been in her shoes only a few months ago. I'd been off the sauce for two months now, but I bent my elbow a lot after the Sunshine case.

13

Skullduggery

Watching Maggie made me curious about her reasons for drowning her sorrows. Dead husband? Dysfunctional family? Or just plain lonely? For sure she had her share of troubles. Nowadays I let my troubles chew up my guts and keep me awake all night. Drowning your problems in booze proved a hopeless cure at least for me. In the morning, I ended up with two problems, rather than one, I still had the troubles and now a hell of a hangover to go with them. And it wasn't cheap either.

She puffed out her cheeks then blew the air from her lungs before she plunked her pudgy frame down on the stool next to mine.

"Hi, Maggie," I said casually.

She looked at me and nodded. "Hi, yourself." Her brow wrinkled. "Who did Bum say you are?"

I smiled. "The guy who's buying." I waved Bum over. He poured more wine in her glass.

"Thanks, buddy, but I still don't know who ya are." She looked away preferring to stare into the mirrored wall. She raised the glass to her lips to take a slow sip. The glass clicked as she set it back on the bar.

I chuckled. "You're one hundred percent right, Maggie. My name's Al Harper. I'm a consultant. Bum asked me here to help him. Seems the place isn't making him independently wealthy."

Maggie's patchy face broke into a grin. After covering her mouth with a fist to bury a smokers cough, she emitted a coarse laugh. She looked at me with blurry eyes and smiled, I think I'd made a new friend. "Good one, Al."

"You here for the mystery game?"

"And the cheap drinks." Her eyes shifted to Pedlar's image in the mirror. "And I enjoy the sporting life." Pedlar caught her looking at him and looked away. His cheeks flushed crimson.

Oh, oh. Friends with privileges. Nice. A lush and a loser. Every bars power couple.

My thoughts were interrupted by the sound of two vehicles arrival in the parking lot. I heard the distinctive crunch of gravel under tires. One sounded heavier than the other, possibly a truck versus a car. Anyone wanting to sneak into the lot without being heard would have a tough time masking their arrival.

The door off the parking lot opened and a stout woman with shoulder length dirty blonde hair walked in carrying two plastic grocery bags in each hand. Her face was round, her skin lined like tanned brown leather. She was dressed in faded blue jeans, sneakers and a forest green windbreaker. She stopped when she spotted me seated at the bar watching her.

"Hi," she said. Her mouth formed a wide smile and her eyes glowed bright with an inner warmth. Finally I'd met someone happy to see me, other than Bum, who actually didn't seem all that pleased to have a stranger in their midst.

"Hi, yourself," I said offering her a crooked grin. I slipped off the stool and approached her. "Let me help you with those bags."

She chuckled. "Well, well, a real gentleman. Those are rare these days." She handed me two of the bags. "I'm headed to the kitchen if you're game."

"Sure," I said then followed her to the lobby where we entered a door beside the front desk. It opened onto a small dining area with six tables complete with place settings and small green vases filled with plastic flowers. We walked through the dining room then through a swinging door into a kitchen.

It wasn't large, but seemed well equipped with a flattop, two commercial ovens, a deep fryer, and a walk-in fridge at the far end of the room. There were various size pots hanging off steel hooks and a cold table beside a butcher block work area. The stainless steel inserts on the cold table were empty.

"Thanks," she said placing the grocery bags on a clean stainless steel table.

She unzipped her coat and slipped it off hanging it off a wooden hook near the door. Under her coat she wore a gray sweat shirt.

"Sure, no problem." I placed the bags I was carrying on the table beside hers and stuck out a hand. "I'm Al Harper."

She took my hand in hers. Her grip was firm. "Nice to meet you, Al. You here for the game?"

I shook my head. "No, Bum asked me to check out his business. I'm a consultant."

Both brown eyebrows on her forehead arched. "Really? I'm the cook. Name's Feather Silca."

"You seem surprised. What about?" I asked.

She smiled thinly then turned away her back to me and began to unpack the bags. "Sorry, it's none of my business, but I gotta get paid ya know."

"Paid?"

"Yeah, Bum's broke. He owes more than the Inn is worth."

Ah, then plot had just become as thick as a slushy on a cold day. "He owe you money?"

She smirked and nodded her attention on the bag of carrots she began to open accompanied by the crinkling sound made by the plastic bag. "Of course, but it's not just wages."

"Oh?"

Skullduggery

She left the work table and went to a row of knifes and kitchen tools resting in slots of a wooden rack hung off the wall above the prep station. She selected a peeler then came back.

"When Bum arrived in town he told everyone, who would listen, about his bar in Boston. He said he paid cash for the Inn and had big plans to improve the place. He also said he needed investors to float the cost of improvements. It all sounded pretty good so I invested my life savings. I accepted the cooks job to keep on eye on my investment." She went to a large dark green plastic garbage can with a black plastic liner inside sitting near a blank wall. It made a scrapping sound when she pulled it across the floor until it was next to her at the work station. She began to peel a carrot over the open maw.

"I gather the improvements didn't go exactly as planned?" She nodded her attention now on the second carrot, the peeler a blur as she stripped off the outer layer, the peelings flying into the garbage can like orange snow. She seemed to be attacking the carrot as if angry. Some people really hate vegetables. Why was she getting so mad?

She was on the third when I asked my follow up question, "What did Bum say about all this?"

She chuckled grimly. "He said he had to pay off some guys back in Boston. He said if he failed to pay them they'd kill him." She stopped peeling and locked eyes with me. "He promised to pay me back as soon as he could." She looked away into the garbage can and began to peel the fourth carrot.

"How long has it been?"

"Six months," she said between gritted teeth.

***

I left the kitchen and walked back into the bar to discover Bum MIA and a man and woman had joined Maggie and Pedlar at the bar. The man set down his glass of beer and stood as I approached.

"Cameron Bell." His rugged face broke into a toothy grin. His teeth were white as new snow and his way too friendly grin made me vaguely uncomfortable. Of course the hair looked like plugs and his pressed blue jeans screamed yuppie. Not my kind of people.

I took his extended hand in mine and regretted it. His grip was as limp as room temperature butter. Bell's eyes fitted to the buxom red head seated on the stool next to Maggie. "This is my wife, Annie. We're in real estate. You looking to move to the area?"

I looked around Bell at his wife and smiled. She offered a tight smile and a nod of her head in greeting.

I'd say Mrs. Bell was early forties trying hard to look early thirties. The perfectly coifed dyed hair, the capped teeth and, like her husband, the pressed blue jeans that were a size too tight, screamed phony. Definitely not my kind of people. Give me a gangster over a phony any day. At least with a gangster you have a shot at seeing the bullet headed for your back.

I looked at Cameron Bell. "Nice to meet you both, Cameron."

He placed a hand on my shoulder. "Call me Cam. Everyone does. Can we buy you a drink?"

"He's on the wagon," said Pedlar from my left side.

Cam arched an eyebrow. "Really? Good for you. Booze is the devils tool. Soda water then?" I nodded then moved to an empty stool beside Mrs. Bell and sat down.

Bell walked to the end of the bar and opened the trap door. Leaving it open he walked down behind the bar until he stood next to the soda dispenser. He glanced at me grinned then looked away to locate a clean glass which he found. He set it on the rubber mat that ran along the bartender side of the bar.

He put in some ice, then using the dispenser filed it with soda water. He glanced at me again. "Lemon or lime?"

I smirked. "Let's live dangerously and go with lime."

Cam emitted a snort. He soon had the glass of bubbling water with a wedge of lime stuck on the rim in front of me.

I picked it up and started to raise it to my lips when a bloodcurdling scream made me freeze. Feather came running into the bar her face white gasping for a breath. "Help!" she said when she came to a standstill her body trembling tears staining her flushed cheeks. She looked about to collapse.

I set down the glass as I leapt to my feel ready to repel all boarders if needed. I moved to stand in front of Feather holding her up by both shoulders. Her watery eyes were wide her expression one of panic. "Calm down, Feather, tell me what's wrong." I spoke gently and deliberately to break through the fear enveloping.

"It's Bum...he's..." Her voice trailed off.

"Where?"

She nodded toward the lobby. She must mean his office. "OK. You stay here. I'll go look." I locked eyes with her. "OK?" She nodded. Annie Bell came up beside me.

I released Feather and made sure Mrs. Bell had her before I hurried to the lobby. I heard the echo of footsteps behind me. I didn't bother looking back thinking it had to be Cam.

The lobby appeared the same as before. Bum's office door was closed and there were no signs of any disturbance. I went to the office door and knocked.

No answer.

"Bum! It's Harper..." I glanced over my shoulder, sure enough Cam Bell was behind me his eyes anxious. "And Cameron Bell."

Silence.

With Feather's words ringing in my memory I knew if I touched the door knob I could contaminate any fingerprint evidence. I went to the front desk and found a box of tissues under the counter. I pulled two from the box and used them to turn the door knob. Then I used the toe of my shoe to push the door open. The light on the desk was left on so I could clearly see Bum's body slumped in his chair. The handle of a knife stuck out from the middle of his chest the blood covered his white shirt. His eyes were open unseeing. The copper smell of blood filled my nose and mouth when I took a step into the room. I stopped and turned my head toward Cam. "Call 911," I said.

Surprisingly Cam shook his head. "No 911 service this far from town. But I'll call the county sheriff's office."

I nodded and he disappeared from the doorway. I turned my attention to the body. Bum clearly wasn't amongst us living anymore. The blade of the weapon was buried to the hilt. I recognized the knife. It matched the set hanging over the prep station I'd seen earlier in the kitchen. I didn't touch anything and left the office making sure to close the door behind me using the tissues.

I took in a deep breath then blew it out to clear the odor of blood from my system. I'd seen a few dead bodies in my day but it never got easier. I'd often thought my application in the psycho killer club had been refused due to a conscience.

I walked over to the front desk and scanned the desk for anything out of place. Everything seemed symmetrical expect a lined pad of paper. The top sheet had been crudely torn off leaving behind a jagged edge. I glanced to my left and saw a door marked employees only and after opening it was behind the desk. I picked up the pad of paper to study it. I narrowed my eyes and saw impressions left by a pen or pencil where someone had pressed hard when writing four words.

The impressions were too faint to make out. Looking up from the paper I saw bunch of mismatched pens and pencils stuffed in a drinking glass on the counter. I pulled a pencil from the nest of writing instruments then used the tip set at an angle to rapidly shade over the impressions. It's a trick as old as papyrus but it works.

The words became clear and my heart skipped a beat. Someone already at the Inn was a killer. I hoped it wasn't the cook. She seemed like the one straight shooter in the place.

I tore off the sheaf of paper and stuffed it into the pocket of my windbreaker then headed for the bar. Instinctively I reached behind my back and brushed the cool steel of the pistol. When I entered the bar I found my five suspects a gathered around a table talking furiously. They fell silent when they saw me coming. My suspect pool was definitely contaminated.

There was an empty chair next to Feather where I plunked myself down with a heavy sigh my hands in my lap beneath the table. I shook my head. "He's dead alright," I said.

"Bum?" asked Annie. I nodded.

Feather moaned and began to sob her face buried in her hands. I suspected she and Bum were more than boss and employee or mutual investors.

"That's awful," breathed Maggie. She stuck her wine glass to her lips and drained it.

I sensed no remorse in her, but since she was a wino with resources it wasn't a conclusive point.

"You get hold of the sheriff's office?" I asked Cam.

"No. The storm has knocked out the phones. We heard on the car radio the road to town is blocked by fallen trees." His eyes flitted to Annie and she nodded confirming his testimony. Too bad she hesitated just enough I knew she playing along with a lie.

What's going on here? I looked at Feather. She'd stopped crying and sat slumped in her chair her face slack with shock. "There's a knife from the set in the kitchen in his chest," I said.

Feather's eyes traveled to mine. "I didn't kill him," she said slowly her voice a hoarse whisper.

I nodded. "Yes, I know." Moving my right hand slowly under my jacket until my fingers were wrapped around the stock of my gun. I smiled at Pedlar. He wasn't trembling nor did he look nervous. In fact he glared at me.

"You think it's me?" he said his tone angry.

"You know, Mr. Pedlar, I'm really not a cop, but I was once a pretty darned good private detective. You told me you knew Bum back in Boston. He said he didn't know you until 2009." I shrugged.

"At first I thought he lied to me until I considered the reasons someone might wish to murder him."

I stood and pulled my gun out from beneath my jacket and let it hang at my side the barrel pointed at the carpet. "Money is often the most powerful motive for murder, but right behind that is love. Or to be more exact break ups and under appreciated love." I smirked. "Ya know, the kind they write country songs about."

"But no one kills for a country song," protested Annie Bell.

I shook my head. "Well, there you'd be wrong, Annie." She scowled at me. "No offense."

I walked toward the bar and sat on a stool facing the four suspects then laid my gun on the bar. I continued. "But I don't think this has anything to do with love." I caught Feather looking at me and offered her a tight smile of reassurance. "I think this has to do with gambling debts. I suspect he lost his bar in Boston when he ran into some debt problems with some not so friendly types. Their interest charges can be deadly."

Pedlar started to rise from his chair. I locked eyes with him and motioned with one hand for him to sit down. I wasn't sure if he'd comply or what I'd do if he didn't, but thankfully he took his seat again.

"I think Pedlar here does know Bum because he works for a loan shark.

He's here to collect the debt, or if he didn't pay...."
I pulled the piece of paper from my jacket pocket. "He wrote this note." I stepped off the stool walked to the table and tossed it in the center. Four sets of eyes stared at the words on the note.

"Huh, Harper, if that's your real name, that's not Pedlar's handwriting," offered Annie.

"Really?" I said already knowing the answer coming and dreading it. "Then who?"

Annie's face went slack and her cheeks turned the color of new snow. "Feather. That's Feather's handwriting."

"How do you know?"

"She gave me a birthday card a few months ago. She makes her d's with a distinctive loop at the end." She looked at Feather. "Why? I thought..."

"He cheated me!" Feather stood forcing her chair tumbled backward landing on the carpet with a thud. I kept my gun at my side watching her. "He cheated us all!" Her voice rose in intensity until she screamed, "He deserved to die!"

I shook my head. "No one deserves to be murdered, Feather," I said.

"I'm leaving you sonofabitch and no one is gonna stop me." I leveled my gun at her. "You gonna shoot an unarmed woman, Harper? Really?" she growled.

She was right of course. I dropped the gun once again to my side. After laughing like a mad woman she fled out the door of the bar. The door thumped closed behind her cutting off the sound of the rain pounding the gravel. I heard the roar of a truck engine roar to life followed by the spray of gravel spat from beneath the tires when she drove away.

I looked at Pedlar. "You do work for a loan shark don't you?" He nodded.

"It seems you're right about everything, Mr. Harper. If that's your real name."

I offered him a crooked smile. "We all practice a little skullduggery, Mr. Pedlar."

Feather wouldn't make it very far.

She was arrested the next day by the sheriff. I'd lost a client but helped to catch a murderer. Of course, I left town the next day, to make sure that I was one step ahead of the cops. Cam and Annie Bell provided the evidence that cinched the case into a nice neat bow. Of course Feather's fingerprints on the knife and the note found in Bum's office put the final nails in her coffin.

When money and love mix, the toxic explosion too often ends in murder, and many, many regrets. Even for me, a former PI named Jazz Stiletto.

The Christmas Club

0012 hours
December 22
In an alley off Hastings Street
Vancouver, Canada

T HE SMOOTH BONE-HANDLE of the knife slipped between his fingers to fall useless to the wet pavement. Twisted shapes formed from inky shadows, surrounded him and mocked his imminent death. Intermittent illumination of headlights from passing cars at both ends of the dark tunnel of brick and mortar was the only light in his failing vision.

As it fell, the knife clattered into the pool of blood that had formed around his mottled gray snakeskin boots.

I love my boots. Funny, there's no pain…can't breathe….

He dropped to his knees. The stench of damp garbage, mingled with his own blood, would be the last thing he would ever smell. Arms, now too weak to stop him, hung limp at his sides when he fell forward. With a sickening smack his face hit the pavement. The rain soaked asphalt felt cool on his skin.

The echo of leather boots against wet pavement receded into the distance … he thought of his mother …

***

0128 hours
December 22, 2004
Hastings Street
Vancouver, Canada

The strobe of flashing lights lit the darkened alley in a swirling mass of white, blue, and red. Other than the low murmur of crime scene technicians securing the area around the body, the only other sounds were the rush of wet tires from passing cars. Their headlights cut the darkness like strobes at the edges of the dank alley. A lone street lamp sitting atop a sagging wooden pole, leaning away from the soot-coated stone wall, was dark. The light in the glass cage burnt out long ago.

City never pays for anything at this end of town, thought Sarah sadly.

Detective Sarah Bascombe stood near the shrouded body, her dusky features a mask of concentration. Her dark eyes flitted momentarily to her partner, Sam Wong, who was squatted on his haunches, his left hand having lifted the gray blanket the first-on-the-scene uniforms had laid over the corpse away.

"What do ya think, Sam?" said Sarah her husky voice echoing off the high stone walls of the narrow alley. The buildings in this part of town dated back to the early twentieth century. The greenish mold in the corners and cracks in the ancient stone were odiferous testament to their age.

"From the look of the wounds around the neck I'd say this guy bled to death," Sam said.

She heard his shoes shuffle to the side, to avoid the sticky, cooling blood that had pooled in places where the pavement had sagged with time. The copper odor of blood permeated the air. She was actually thankful the smell blocked to usual odors of rot and decay in this dank, dirty alley.

"Something very sharp, and very thin, went through the neck—it severed the carotid artery...." She heard him patting what she knew to be the two back pockets of the dead man's blue jeans.

"I got something."

Sarah glanced up from her notebook and eyed the wallet in Sam's gloved hand. She smirked and shook her head. At least he remembered to wear his gloves. Rookies.

She closed her worn leather notebook with a flip, and then slipped into the right pocket of her soft chocolate-brown suede jacket. The feel of the suede brushed gently against her skin — the jacket was a gift from Eddie — last Christmas.

"Give it to me," she said.

Sam walked over and handed her the wallet. She pulled out her penlight she kept in a vinyl holder on her belt, and turned it on. Flipping open the wallet as if it were a Star Trek communicator she revealed the vics drivers license in its little plastic-coated window.

Alan Cuthbert, age thirty-one. She noted the late Mr. Cuthbert's address...

A knot formed in her stomach. Opening the billfold, she saw there were a number of bills. Green and red. That meant twenties and fifties. Her hand trembled slightly as she handed the wallet back to Sam. This death wasn't a robbery.

"Count the money," she said. Replacing the flashlight into its holder she pulled out her cell phone from its holster also on her belt.

Moving moved away from Sam, in order to be out of earshot (he was mumbling under his breath as he counted the bills), she flipped open the phone and hit a pre-programmed number.

It rang twice at the other end before a sleepy male voice answered. "Highgate."

"It's me. We found Alan Cuthbert dead in an east end alley tonight."

"When?" said the male voice suddenly sounding alert.

"I'm here now." Her eyes flitted side-to-side scanning the shadows for movement. Nothing. "I'm with my partner."

"Ok. I'll call the medical examiner, and meet you at his office first thing in the morning."

"Ed?"

"Yeah."

"I'm scared."

"Yeah. I know."

***

0800 Hours
December 23, 2004
Vancouver Police Headquarters

The next morning Sarah arrived at the station, after a fitful sleep on the leatherette couch in her west end apartment.

The Christmas Club

She wore the same clothes from the night before. Her cool, pale hands cupped a steaming cup of Starbucks strongest.

The medical examiners office was in the basement of the Main Street police headquarters. The red brick building dated back to the '50's, a time when many of its current occupants were either in diapers, or not yet born. Rumor had it that if you removed the worn burgundy carpets from the floors the number of holes drilled through to install data and telephone communication lines would resemble Swiss cheese. Sarah often wondered when the building would implode. And she hoped she was at home when it happened.

Fat chance of that. After pressing the keyless entry button on her key ring a loud beep echoed off the crumbling brick walls of the old station. It signaled the door locks engaging on her car.

Once inside the building the sudden change in temperature caused her to shiver. The winter air outside was wet and cold. A strong wind was blowing this morning through the tall steel and glass towers that stood in stark contrast to the ancient cedars and firs that once populated where the city had sown its roots.

Constable Phil Singh sat behind the bulletproof glass at the reception desk.

His navy blue uniform shirt crisp, the sleeves ironed razor sharp. He smiled as he saw her enter. He smelled of coffee and cigarettes his two vices.

"Hi, Sarah," he said brightly. "You look a little beat today."

She nodded. "Yeah. I was up most of the night. We found a body off Hastings in an alley."

"Ya know, Sarah, you guys gotta get a bloodhound like me into homicide. I could crack the case in a day."

She smiled. "Yeah, right Sherlock." Moving to the door to the left of reception area, she wrapped her long fingers around the door handle. "Now buzz me in, will ya. I have to talk to the doc."

"You got it." The buzzer sounded and Sarah pulled on the burnished steel door handle. The door opened easily.

"Merry Christmas," said Phil.

"I thought Sikhs didn't believe in our pagan holidays?"

"Everyone believes in Santa —"

Sarah's dry laughter echoed in the interior hallway as the door closed behind her. Walking a short distance she quickly arrived outside the smoked glass door marked, MEDICAL EXAMINER.

She held her breath, to steady her nerves, and then walked inside.

The Christmas Club

The door rattled as it closed behind her.

The familiar mix of cleaning chemicals and stale coffee filled her nostrils. There was desk and two chairs, which were covered in loose papers scattered across the pale oak surface, as if by some errant eggbeater. A last-generation computer sat unused on the desk. The desk was not exactly ergonomic, but then the medical examiner was not the kind of man who worried about such things.

Guy gives me the creeps.

A door at the back of the room opened with a creaking noise and Ed Highgate stepped into the room followed by the white lab coat of Doc Albright. Sarah knew they had just come from examining her second cousins corpse.

***

"Sarah," Ed said looking up. His voice, a mellow tenor, was edged with tension, when he saw her standing watching him and Albright enter. Puppy sad eyes, that were as calm as a summer evening, seemed to penetrate her soul. Those eyes are trouble.

She had known it the day she had first met the man. Mom always said, 'Watch the eyes. They're the window to the soul'.

His tanned complexion and chiseled chin were set in a grim expression. Instead of his usual chief-of-detectives uniform, tie and jacket, he was wearing faded blue jeans, and a loose jean shirt that hung over his narrow waist. His rough hands were buried in the pockets hidden beneath the billowing shirt. She spotted his black leather jacket thrown haphazardly over one of the chairs near the back wall.

"...like I was saying, just like the others..." Albright's high-pitched voice cut through her like nails on a chalkboard. Albright pushed his black framed glasses up his nose when he noticed her standing watching them. The liver spots on the backs of his pale, wrinkled hands looked larger than she recalled. It had been a while for which she was grateful.

"Detective," he said nodding, his gray eyes clear and cool.

She nodded then sat on one of the pine chairs. Albright sat behind his ancient desk. The old oak chair squeaked loudly in the musty air as his weight hit it. Ed remained standing.

Sarah took a sip from her cup, the scent of roasted beans filled her mouth and nose as the bitter black coffee hit her taste buds. I needed that.

"I gather this is the same as before?" she said her eyes never leaving Albrights withered features.

Wasn't the man ever going to retire?

"As I was telling the Chief here, this man was killed in the same manner as the victims from the past two years." Albright's voice was steady and he showed no emotional reaction to what he had just said.

In contrast, she felt her heart freeze in her chest. This time it was personal. This time it was one of her family.

***

For the past two years, on three consecutive days, December 22nd, 23rd, and 24th there had been three murders. Each of the victims were members of the same family. The families were the wealthy elite, and all from the same section of the city, the West Side of Vancouver.

Alan was, or rather had been, her second cousin. She didn't know him very well. Her side of the family was considered the black sheep of the line. Her Dad had lost his inheritance in the market "adjustment" of 1987.

The problem was the next victim would be tonight, and it could be anyone in her family. And there would be another on Christmas Eve before this was over.

They had tried everything to stop these murders. So far, they had found no clues. Nothing. And the frustration was showing at the seams, both from within and outside the department.

All they knew for sure was the killer was a pro. No doubt about it. Someone paid for these hits and pros didn't come cheap. Was it competitors? Jealous lovers?

The only common denominator was that each of the three series of victims were from the same family. There just were no other connections that they could find.

No mistresses, at least that anyone would admit. Even if they knew about infidelity, they weren't about to talk about it.

"Surgical steel is a remarkable thing," Albright said. "As was the case in the last two events a thin steel rod, composed of surgical steel was used to penetrate the neck of the victim. This severed the carotid artery and the victim bled out within minutes. Because the damage was inflicted inside the throat, the victim drowned in his own blood, even as it spilled out of the small incisions in the neck and from the mouth. Once a major artery is opened, the heart will pump as much blood as possible through the wound. Remarkable —"

"There's nothing remarkable about it —" Sarah's anger spilled out of her.

Ed held up one hand. "Whoa, Sarah. The doc is only trying to help."

She grumbled and took another sip of the rich aromatic coffee, which was now cold.

"Doc, we need to know where such an instrument could be made. Is it standard issue for you medico types?"

Albright buried his gnarled hands in the pockets of his lab coat and rocked backward in the squeaky chair. "As I said last year, and the year before, to your predecessor, no such device exists. It had to be made special for this job."

"So, we're looking for a professional killer that has a custom made surgical steel pin designed to kill people," said Ed.

Sarah thought Ed was kidding, but one look in his eyes told her he wasn't joking. She'd seen the look before. "Ed," said Sarah. "I checked with all surgical steel manufacturers North America wide last year and nothing."

"So we have no leads." Ed said, a frown marring his handsome features, the frustration clear on his face. "I was hired to get to the bottom of these murders, and by God I'm going to do just that."

He turned to face Sarah. "Sarah, call the cowboys, Customs, and the U.S. guys, and tell them to put out watch- for a custom made surgical steel pin. The doc will give you the probable dimensions. I'm gonna have a chat with the chief. I know he'll want the latest."

Sarah nodded. She didn't have the heart to tell him they did the same thing two years running and nothing was ever found. The killer did his nasty work and disappeared until the next year.

***

Sarah placed the phone in its cradle and made a quick note on her screen about her conversation with the officer-in-charge at US Customs and Border Protection at Vancouver Airport pre-clearance. He assured her they would keep a close watch for anyone carrying such a device.

Her phone rang again interrupting her thoughts. "Bascombe."

"This is the front desk. We have a woman here says she's the mother of the vic from last night. The constable's voice sounded world-weary. Phil must've gone home. The gold colored clock on her desk said it was after six, again. "She's demanding to see someone…"

"Ok. Send her up."

Sarah hung up without waiting for an acknowledgment. With both hands flat on her paper-strewn desk, she pushed herself up and ran a hand through her tangled shoulder length hair. God, what a mess.

She walked to the elevators just as it arrived. The doors parted to reveal a gray-haired woman dressed in a knee length navy blue dress, with white wavy trim along the hemline. Her gray mottled tweed over coat was unbuttoned, and she was clutching a gray leather handbag. The clothes were expensive so Sarah knew there were troubled waters ahead.

The older woman led her across the squad room, as if she were in charge. Which maybe she was.

Sarah followed silently behind, her eyes watching the head of artificially curled white-gray back to her desk. She sat down and waited for the deluge to start. The elderly woman's perfume wafted about her like a cloud. It had that expensive French scent. This woman was money. The way she fidgeted told Sarah the woman probably has cocktails with the chief at the Vancouver Club Christmas party. She'd certainly never been in here before.

Odd. I don't recognize her —

"I'm here to complain," said the woman, her voice sharp.

Without it being offered, she sat down on the simulated leather cushion of the chair next to Sarah's desk. Her lips were thin and bloodless. Her sallow cheeks marred by bright-red blush that was liberally applied to disguise an unhealthy appearance. Regardless, her makeup did not distract from the intense gaze of the worldly-eyes that seemed to look right through Sarah, as if the older woman had x-ray vision.

"Do I know you?" asked Sarah.

The woman eased back in the chair until her ramrod straight back rested against the chair back, her Gucci handbag clutched in withered hands, tight across her lap. "I'm your Uncle William's sister. My name is Mrs. Agnes Cuthbert. And, young lady I'm here to complain —"

Hmmm, interesting. "About what?" Sarah folded her hands in her lap and gazed at her never-before-seen Aunt Agnes. It would seem she knows who I am.

Her estranged aunt's eyes went wide in surprise, and then shifted to annoyance as her eyes narrowed. Sarah decided she better shift gears herself. "Well, Aunt Agnes I assume you're here because of Allan's murder —"

"Murder!?" The makeup did not cover whatever blood remained in Agnes's system, as her face became the color of fireplace ash.

43

Sarah silently chastised herself. *This business must be jading me. Often when people come to see a homicide detective she assumed they know their loved one was* —

"Sorry, Aunt Agnes. I meant to say we're treating Allan's death as suspicious, until we rule out all possibilities —"

Agnes shook her head slowly and her gaze dropped to Sarah's desk. A lone silvery tear escaped to travel down her withered cheek. Sarah almost felt sorry for the old woman—almost. Everyone was a suspect, until the case was closed.

Sam came in the room whistling jingle bells. Sarah caught his eye and he stopped, his cheeks reddening. Fortunately, Agnes did not seem to notice the younger detective's arrival.

Sam sat down behind his desk pretending to read his e-mail. His dark eyes drifted in her direction every few seconds.

"I'm very sorry about your loss. But I have to tell you this is not the first case we've had of this type —"

Agnes sharp eyes shot up to look through her as though Sarah were a prize mare at the finest breeding farm in the valley. "Yes. I know. That is why I am here. The ladies at my club have been henning about this for weeks."

The image of blue hairs sitting at square card tables pecking the tables as if they were chickens in the barnyard passed through Sarah's mind. She managed to suppress the image, keeping her expression bland.

"We want — no, we demand protection," Agnes said firmly.

Sarah stared at the old woman for several seconds. "We don't know who to protect exactly. As you know our family is very large. It would take every constable we have to protect all of them."

Agnes' eyes narrowed. "I only care about…" her eyes flitted toward Sam, who had his eyes buried on his computer screen, but Sarah knew his ears were set to seek and destroy.

"..certain members of my family."

Sarah had learned long ago to ignore the insults from the so-called <u>well-heeled</u> members of her extended family. They were just a bunch of elitist snobs, but something about Agnes's words tickled her natural suspicious nature.

"What about Allan? Was he in the 'certain', or 'not-so-certain' class?"

Agnes' gaze went hard, and her frail body visibly stiffened. "Allan was…unacceptable. We have our standards."

45

Sarah's eyebrows went up. "Oh, really. And who exactly is we?"

A small smile drifted over Agnes's features, accompanied by a burst like a July firecracker behind her eyes. "I think you, of all people, know exactly what I mean."

Sarah nodded. I've had enough of this bitch.

She pushed back her chair with her lean legs and stood, her hands instinctively smoothing her black jeans, as if she were washing herself off.

"We'll get back to you about the protection, after I confer with my superiors. And once we find Allan's killer, you'll be the first to know."

Agnes rose to her feet, her expression self-important, turned her back to Sarah and walked away. Her Italian leather heels tapped loudly against the ancient tile floor. "I'll find my way out, detective." She said detective as if the word left a bad taste in her mouth, which maybe it did. Civil service was not something the Cutherbert family tree thought of as a useful profession

Sarah followed the old woman's progress, all the while considering whether to pull out her 9mm and put one in the old woman's back. Someone has to put her kind out of its misery.

If it were a consolation, at least Allan wouldn't have to put up with any more of the Cuthbert pressure, as her Dad had once referred to that family's less that noble trait.

Finally, the old woman disappeared behind the elevators doors. Only then did Sarah drop her gaze to her young partner, who had a lopsided grin pasted to his bronze face. "Family problems?" he said.

Sarah frowned and sat back down behind her desk, the breath she'd been holding escaping into the too warm air. Like her mother always said, "If you don't have anything good to say about someone, say nothing". Thanks, Mom.

***

2223 hours
Dec 23, 2004
Vancouver Police Headquarters

Sarah's cell phone song woke her from a troubled sleep; she had changed it to jingle bells in honor of the season. Her head rested on a case folder on her desk, the pages damp from the trickle of drool that came from the side of her mouth. One bloodshot eye opened slowly. A soft moan escaped her dry lips, and she cleared her throat.

She sat back in her chair. Pinching the bridge of her nose, to remove the sleep from her eyes, between slender, dark fingers, she reached for the cell phone on her belt.

Blinking twice she flipped it open and brought it to her right ear. "Yes," she said her voice husky from lack of sleep. Dark eyes shifted to the half-eaten egg salad on brown Sam had brought her from Penny's Cafe around the corner from the station.

"Auntie Sarah? It's Philip."

Philip? Her sisters youngest. A tow headed fifteen-year-old with a mind that imaginations were made for.

"Philip, how are you…why are you calling?" she said without thinking. She cringed inside.

"Auntie, why are you working so late?"

Out of the mind of teenagers. Oh, to be in high school again.

"It's the nature of the job, Philip. Sorry. I'm a little busy…" she picked up the half-eaten sandwich and her stomach heaved at the god-awful smell coming from the stale mayonnaise. She tossed it in the steel trashcan next to her desk, her nose wrinkled in disgust. She looked around and saw that Sam was gone. She was alone in the squad room.

Philip laughed brightly in her ear, and she felt her heart ache for what might have been. She pushed away her regrets.

"Auntie, I wanted to call you because your Christmas package arrived today. I might not be able to reach you on Christmas day so I thought I'd call you now." Sarah looked up at the red digital numbers on the alarm clock she kept on her desk. It was almost ten-thirty…

"Philip, isn't it a little past your bed time?"

Philip laughed again. "Auntie, I'm not ten years old any more ya know. Besides, I had to watch A Christmas Carol. Ya know, the olden days one."

Sarah nodded. "Yes. I know the one."

"Anyway, I gotta go now. Love you, Auntie. Merry Christmas."

"I love you too, Philip and Merry Christmas. Tell your Mom and Dad I'll call on Christmas day." I hope.

She really didn't want to talk with her family right now. They might ask questions about her current case. The danger would be over after Christmas Eve. However, she hoped to find the killer within the next twenty-four hours, or they'd have to wait until next year. So far, they had so little go on it seemed all but hopeless.

"Okay, Auntie. Bye."

The Christmas Club

Sarah flipped her cell phone closed. It sang again immediately. She flipped it open, dreading in her gut that it was her sister, Joy. It wasn't.

"Sarah, it's Sam. We found another one."

***

2248 hours
December 23, 2004
Hastings at Burrard Street

She arrived at the scene to find Sam and Ed already on site. A gaggle of patrol cars, the coroner's meat wagon, and an ambulance were gathered in the intersection of Burrard and Hastings. Uniforms were directing what little traffic there was around an area marked with yellow police tape and orange rubber pylons.

Sarah saw a television truck, and that red haired reporter who anchored the weekend news, standing behind the barricades that had been set up. The pretty young woman's expression was anxious as she tried in vain to get closer, attempting to bypass the giant uniform that blocked her way. They were going to have to tell them something. The killer went to a lot of trouble to advertise this one.

A patrol unit called it in. The office towers in the downtown core form steel and glass canyons, and during the days before Christmas, are deserted and quiet, especially at night. The hustle and bustle of office workers give way to a quiet stillness. And, the sea air from the harbor again reclaimed the modern canyons, replacing the fumes of the automobiles, trucks, and buses of modern city life.

The array of red, blue, and white emergency lights made the glass towers sparkle like Christmas trees. Visible from the intersection was Canada Place, with its magnificent sails lit with bright red, green, blue, and yellow lights. It shot into the cold night sky, a stark reminder of the seasonal flavor that had enveloped the city. Good will to men. Nice idea, she thought.

In normal circumstances, they would have said this was a nice night, except for the victim's corpse hidden beneath the tan tarp lying on the damp pavement.

Sarah walked to where Ed and Sam stood. Sam glanced up from his notebook and gave her tight smile as she approached them. Ed's features remained passive, his dark, sad eyes staring at her. His notebook was one in his hand, and the silver pen she had given him for his last birthday, hovered over the page in the other.

"What have we got?" she said.

The Christmas Club

Sam handed her a man's black leather wallet. His eyes shifted to it and it was clear he wanted her to open it. She held it her stomach in knots. Who was it this time? Which member of her family?

She flipped it open to the driver's license window and saw the picture. The world dropped away from beneath her. She felt woozy and her knees trembled.

"You okay?" said Ed. Sam moved to grab her by the elbow to steady her.

She swallowed hard then said, "Yeah. I'm fine."

Max. It was Max Pierrepont. Her ex-husband.

***

Max had once been one of the top investment advisors in the city, until the market went south. First in '87, then again during the dot com crash. Not that her side of the family had much left after '87, but Sarah was certain her extended family had lost a considerable sum during that little 'market adjustment'. And, she was sure they would've lined up Max as the fall guy. An outsider. An ex-pat American who married into the family. She loved him once.

Background checks on the late Allan Cuthbert established he had also been working for the same investment brokerage at the time of his death.

Somehow, she doubted this was a coincidence. Could this all be that simple?

She needed to delve deeper into the records of the other victims. If it were true, how had they missed it?

Her eyes flitted to Ed who stood near the body talking to Doc Albright. Curious. Why was the old coroner out here so late?

Ed stopped talking when he saw her approaching them. Every instinct in her body told her something was very wrong.

"Same MO as the others, doc?" she asked.

Albright gave her a dismissive stare. "Yes."

She patted Ed lightly on the back. "Can we have a word — in private?"

Ed nodded and they walked away together out of earshot of everyone on the scene. There was the snap of leather against wet pavement, as the blood rushed through her ears like a torrent of a rushing tide. Her heart beat faster in her chest. A flavor like that of sour milk permeated her taste buds.

This can't be happening to me again. When she judged they were far enough away she spun on Ed and said, her voice a hoarse whisper, "What's going on? Tell me right now." She crossed her arms across her chest.

The Christmas Club

Dark eyes, normally placid as a mountain lake at dawn, withered under her steady gaze. His eyes dropped to the pavement. The broad muscular shoulders she longed to hold drooped.

"The chief called me. He wants you off the case. And so do I." His eyes popped up and looked into to hers the care and concern written on his tanned face.

"What? I thought we talked about this..." He promised me. "...I'm going to see this thing through —"

"The chief insists." His deep voice was urgent, and the pale scar on his right cheek whitened as his jaw line visibly tightened.

She shook her head and short snort of disgust escaped her lips. "Fine." I don't care what he, or the chief says I'm sure who's behind this. And I'm gonna get them. All of them.

***

1828 hours
December 24, 2004
W 18th Avenue, Vancouver

Ed and she agreed she would take a few days off and come back the day after New Years. Sam would take the lead on the investigation.

Sam said he had a lead on a member of the Red Eagles gang, a punk named Billy Cho. Billy was the enforcer for the Red Eagles, and it was well known he often hired out to make hits for rich clients. As far as they knew, he'd never made a hit for anyone outside the Chinese community. The Chinese never discuss their affairs outside their own community. They take care of their own.

Sarah knew the lead was a dead-end, but they were grasping at straws. She on the other hand knew she needed to take care of her own, before another member of her family died.

The house looked deserted when she pulled up in front. The ancient oaks that lined both side of the street had long ago dropped their leafs. They stood like multi-armed guardians and obscured some of the houses on either side.

Situated in an old money neighborhood, Aunt Agnes' house, a Cape Cod style, the front bone white, and a red brick chimney running up one side of the two-story building, was typical of the type of homes in this section of the city. The wood trim that ran the length and breadth of the structure was the finest money could buy, and even in winter, the lawn looked as if it had been trimmed with a nail clipper, one blade at a time.

A lot better shack than my west end apartment, that's for sure.

Picking up the hand written notes she'd made when she called her sister for the address, she confirmed it was the right house. Her aunt had sent Joy and her family a Christmas card. Joy must be of the certain acceptable variety.

Scanning the street, she saw there were a few cars parked on either side. All appeared empty of occupants. Good.

Instinctively, she checked her 9mm hidden beneath her suede jacket, sheathed in its leather shoulder holster. A wave of reassurance washed over her when her fingers touched the cool of the molded butt of the pistol. No one is gonna screw with me today.

She stepped onto the street, and closed the door with a slam that echoed through the leafless trees on the deserted street. The slight breeze from the west hit her in the face, carrying with it the smell of smoke and rotting leaves.

As she came to the front door of her aunt's house, she tapped the doorbell button lightly with her right index. finger. The doorbell chimed, and what had to be a small dog began to yap incessantly. Great. An ankle biter.

The distinct sound of footsteps against wood floors, and Aunt Agnes' voice shushing her dog, whose name was apparently Princess, came through the door.

Finally, it opened to reveal her aunt dressed in a knee-to-neck sky-blue dress and black leather heels. Her silver-gray hair was stacked neatly in tight curls atop her head, as if she'd just come from the hairdresser. No one has the right to look this good. Under one arm Agnes held a small dog, a Maltese.

The look of surprise in the old woman's eyes was why Sarah was here. "Didn't expect to see me again so soon, did you Aunt Agnes?"

The old woman's eyes changed to her usual controlled calm, but Sarah could see in her gray eyes her aunt wanted to slam the door shut in her face. "I don't understand —"

With her hand flat on the door, Sarah pushed her way past the old woman, forcing her to take a step back.

"Well, I never! I'm going to call your superiors —"

Sarah smiled and withdrew her pistol from the shoulder holster. "Don't sound so innocent, Auntie. You know perfectly well why I'm here —"

Sarah moved further down the hallway, past the fine cherry wood and dark-stained oak end tables, each with a polished brass lamp resting on it.

Paintings of pastoral scenes of green fields and brown horses lined the walls, until at last she came to the front sitting room. What she saw there surprised her.

"I'm going to call the chief. Immediately —" Agnes said behind her.

Sarah spun and leveled her pistol at the old woman, whose hand was frozen in mid-air reaching for an antique style telephone sitting atop a half moon-shaped cherry wood table. "Don't do that, old woman."

Agnes dropped her hands to her sides, her steady gaze watchful yet unflinching. Not much was gonna scare this old broad.

"Let's mingle with your guests." She motioned with the pistol for Agnes to move past and ahead of her, into the sitting room.

On the overstuffed couches of gold and burgundy sat three silver haired women. Fine oriental silk throw rugs lay under the two large coffee tables in front of the couches. A large gilded frame surrounding a gleaming mirror almost covered one entire wall.

The ladies appeared to be perfectly quaffed, like their hostess, and each wore clothes that would be the envy of runway models from Paris to New York. In their laps, they each held an ornately painted fine china cup.

The room smelled of orange pekoe and sweet cinnamon.

Agnes walked ahead of her, her manner calm and her head held high. The three women sat unfazed by Sarah's appearance, as if it were quite ordinary to have a police detective in the room, with her gun out.

"This is my niece —"

"Estranged niece," corrected Sarah.

Agnes nodded and a small sighed escaped her thin bloodless lips. "Yes, of course — my estranged niece, Sarah Bascombe." She waved one hand toward the three ladies. "These ladies are members of my club."

"Club?" Sarah flicked the safety on her gun then holstered it. None of these four old women was, or even could be, a threat.

"Yes. We decide what's best for the community-at-large." Agnes moved to one of the long burgundy overstuffed couches, where she sat down next to one of the ladies wearing a forest green knee-length dress. The regal looking woman wore a choker of brilliant white pearls around her elegant, pale neck. The woman's emerald eyes gazed unflinchingly at the interchange between the two estranged relatives.

Agnes placed Princess next to her on the couch; the small dog curled up next to her thigh, then picked up a teacup, off a coaster from the gleaming cherry wood coffee table in front of her, and took a sip. She shook her head.

"I'm rather disappointed in you, Sarah. I would have thought you would have guessed by now."

Sarah felt a cold chill run through her. The investments went sour. The victims all either worked for the same investment firm, or they had invested in it…a lot of people, just like these took a bath because of the victims negligence…the file said so, but…this group of rich bitches had those responsible murdered. Simple. Money, power…no…there was something else…something much more sinister…but what?

Her cell phone rang in the silence, broken only by the incessant ticking coming from an antique grandfather clock set against one wall. Sarah plucked the cell phone from her belt and flipped it open. "Bascombe."

"Sarah, it's Sam. I checked the list of vics from the past three Christmas' and found a hole in your theory. Skyler Investments never had an employee named Serge Gordey. Nor was there any record of anyone by that name having being an investor with them. According to his surviving relatives,

Serge only invested in blue chips, like banks or IBM. Very low risk stuff that he watched himself, and bought through an old time broker at one of the local brokerage firms. They also told me he was gay, and they wanted to know if we ever found his lover —"

Sarah snapped her phone shut. Max was gay. Was Allan? Were all of the victims gay?

Sarah stared at her aunt, who wore a tolerant smile on her pale face, like someone whose pet had just learned a new trick.

"Now do you understand?" said Agnes, her eyes gazing over the rim of the teacup. Had she heard? Impossible…still.

Sarah shook her head. "No. That can't be right…"

Agnes placed her teacup back on its coaster, and then her pale hands smoothed the ruffled dress in her lap. "We are the moral compass of this community. Think of us as the surgeons exorcising a tumor.

Every Christmas we give our community a gift for three successive days." Agnes paused as if she were searching for the right phrase. "We're a sort of Christmas club and tonight will be number three."

Agnes' eyes drifted toward the grandfather clock. "I would say, in about an hour, this year's lot will be finished. Until next year …"

Sarah shook her head. "No. You're murderers — all of you." She scanned the passive faces that stared back at her.

Agnes laughed, and the other three women smiled warmly. "How would you ever prove we were involved? Don't you think we have those bases covered? The money is untraceable, and our Mr. Red will be on a plane tonight."

"Mr. Red?"

"Maybe I should join the police force," said Agnes mockingly.

A hired killer. That made sense. These bitches plotted murder all year and then hired someone to take out the garbage. Wealthy families probably even paid them to rid themselves of gay relatives. Agnes was right, without the evidence, and the hit man, how was she going to prove any of this?

…it's a shame, really the last one tonight is so young, but it was my turn this year to clean our family name —"

Sarah thought hard. Who in her family was gay? Who? Like she was an expert. She hadn't known Max was gay until five years after they were married.

She ran Agnes' words in her mind. Young? Gay? Philip? No, God…please no…not Philip!

"Philip Fahey?"

Agnes stared back at her, her expression passive her eyes devoid of emotion. Sarah pulled out her pistol again and flipped off the safety with her thumb. Though she didn't need to, she cocked the hammer to emphasize her point.

Through gritted teeth she said, "You will tell me what I want to know, or I swear to God I will shoot you."

Agnes waved away the threat. "I'm an old woman. Go ahead. I'm doing this for our family's purification."

"Have you ever seen what a nine millimeter bullet does to the human body? I assure you, it's not a pretty sight —"

Agnes shrugged.

Sarah pointed the pistol at Princess. "If you don't tell me, I'm going to turn the <u>Princess</u> here into a fluffy duster."

Agnes frowned. She put down her cup and placed her withered hands flat on her knees. "You don't have enough time —"

"Let me decide — "Sarah ran over the route in her mind to get to Joy's place from here. <u>I can make it</u>. Her fingers tightened around the stock of the pistol and her finger tightened on the trigger.

"Yes, Philip —"

Sarah redirected the pistol at the large mirror and pulled the trigger. There was loud boom followed by the shattering of glass and a large hole appeared in the center of the mirror with a spider-web-like nest of cracks radiating from the epicenter. The dog yelped, jumped to the floor and scurried away, her nails clicking loudly like the report of a machine gun, until she disappeared around a wall.

"Why did you do that?!" said Agnes who had shot up from the couch, her eyes angry.

"It was better than Princess?" Sarah turned and ran for the door. As she ran, she pulled her cell phone and dialed Joy's home number.

She reached her car door as the line connected. Holding the phone to one ear, she fumbled in her coat pocket for her keys, until she had them in her trembling fingers. The line rang, and rang, and rang… no answer. She flipped her phone closed then placed it in its holster. Where could they be?

The green digital clock on her dash came on when she started the engine. 6:45. <u>Church</u>. They were at church. Every Christmas Eve.

Sarah grabbed the cool plastic handle of the floor shift, shoved it into drive, then stomped hard on the gas pedal.

The four-cylinder engine roared and the car leapt away from the curb, like a grey hound after the rabbit.

The Honda slewed to the left, but she managed to get it under control before it slid into a parked car. Sarah drove with one hand as she pulled her phone again off her belt and hit the quick dial number she'd programmed for Sam.

The young detective's voice came on immediately. "Wong —"

"Sam. Thank God. It's Sarah. I know I hung up on you, but I had to get to my car and try to warn my sister. My nephew Philip is the next target. A hit man is on his way to his church right now. It's on the corner of 51st and Fraser. Fraser Baptist. Sam? You got me?"

"Yeah, except I have the hit-man in custody — well not exactly in custody. He's dead —"

"What? That can't be right — Agnes said —"

"The old lady? Nope. Sorry, she's wrong. We found the murder weapon in his apartment."

Sarah slowed her car as she came to a red light. There were few cars on the road tonight so she was making good time. She was already at Broadway and Main. Something was wrong with this. It can't be Billy — it just can't —

She tried to recall the faces of the women in her aunt's sitting room.

Mrs. Rabin, in the pink pastel with matching shoes, Mrs. Blasie, in her forest green dress, and Mrs. Langmack in royal blue. She recalled reading in the case files, from the last two years series of murders, that the victims were members of those three families. It suddenly dawned on her; Agnes lied. There weren't going to be any more murders. If they had nearly completed what they set out to do. Then only one more remained…Philip.

She looked both ways. No cars. She hit the gas pedal hard and the tires beneath her spun on the wet pavement until, with a fishtail, the Honda shot through the intersection.

"You've got the wrong man," said Sarah. "I know Ed wants to close the case, but the job hasn't been finished yet. I'm going to be at that church in the next ten minutes. I'd suggest you get over there." She flipped the phone closed, turned off the power, and tossed it into the back seat.

***

When she arrived at the church, she pulled across the street, going the wrong way on Fraser Street, and came to a screeching halt in front. Stone steps led to the heavy oak doors the guarded the old church.

She threw the car door leaving the engine running, and ran up the stairs, taking two at a time. Her mouth was dry and the air smelled of burning wood. She pulled her pistol out as she came to twin polished wood doors.

It was quiet. There should be music… She moved to stand beside the door with a typed note taped to it. The note said to use this door to enter. The other door was apparently locked. She pressed her back against the locked door, her gun held in both hands, the barrel pointed up.

Reaching across she felt the cool of the hard polished wood handle. She pulled hard and the door shot open. She crouched low her pistol barrel pointed at the door. Nothing, no sound, no movement. The door closed with soft thud.

Time to earn my paycheck.

Moving to stand beside the door, she thrust herself through the open doorway, dropping to her belly, the pistol held out in front of her like a pointer. In the carpeted lobby, on either side of two interior doors, stood a man and a woman. Both steel haired seniors, their expressions coned shaped, twin pairs of eyes wide with astonishment. Both were dressed in their Sunday best. They each held sheaves of colored paper.

Sarah nodded to them, but they remained staring at her unmoving, not speaking. She noted the perspiration on their furrowed brows and recognized the fear behind the startled expressions.

Agnes had called ahead. Damn her. I should have thought of that…

She rolled away from the two stricken seniors until; she lay hear a wall. She moved to her knees all the while keeping her eyes scanning for threats. Nothing.

She stood up then moved to the opposite wall next to the open doors. The woman stood beside her, her gray-blue eyes flitting toward the open doors. Sarah took a deep breath into her lungs then, crouching low, ran for the opened doors hoping she would surprise the hit man.

More likely, I'll be shot, but I have to take the chance.

She broke through bursting into the foyer her gun at the ready. The sanctuary was visible through panes of clear glass. The congregation sat on the benches facing forward. There on pulpit, at the front of the church, a gleaming gold cross on the high wall behind them, stood Philip and the hit man — or should I say hit-woman.

Long blonde curls fell over the narrow shoulders of a black head-to-toe skin-tight outfit of a woman, who Sarah guessed was about thirty-five. Her face was a mask of calm, and in her left gloved hand, she held what looked like a silver stick. Her free hand gripped Philip's neck.

The killing device was pressed into Philip's neck, but had not yet pierced his tender young flesh. I hate being right.

Racing down the aisle, she ran toward her nephew and his assailant, her heart beating hard in her chest, the pistol pointed at the blonde woman. She had gotten about half way when a voice demanded her attention.

"Another step and he's dead." The husky timber of the voice made her come to halt, but she kept her pistol aimed at the woman's head.

"You kill him. I kill you," Sarah said, her voice echoing off the high walls of the sanctuary.

"You're willing to sacrifice him?" said the woman, a whisper of a smile danced over her full red lips.

Philip's frightened eyes pleaded with Sarah. What do I do? My sister..._

She pulled the trigger. A loud boom cut the air. Spent gunpowder replaced the scent of wood polish.

The bullet struck Philip in his right leg shattering the bone.

He screamed and hunched forward. Surprised, the blonde killer pulled the surgical steel pin away from Philip's neck when he leaned forward to grasp his wounded leg. It was enough.

Sarah fired again. The bullet entered the woman's body in the center of her pale forehead. With a sickening popping noise, the bullet hit the carved relief on the wall behind them. It carried with it bloody brain matter that splattered over the altar behind them. The woman fell backward due to the force of the bullet, landing with a dull thud on the carpeted floor.

Screams, mingled with gasps of terror, split the air replacing the sound of the shots report.

Philip moaned loudly, bloody fingers grasped his shattered leg. He rolled back and forth, his face a mask of agony. Sirens in the street outside screamed. Help was on the way.

Sarah glanced over to where her sister Joy sat. Joy's delicate features were a myriad of conflicting emotion. She sat unmoving, shock held her in place. Finally, her pale brown eyes turned to lock on Sarah's.

Her husband, Kenn had already moved to help his son, his cell phone out calling for an ambulance.

"Why?" Joy whispered, amplified by the acoustics of the sanctuary.

"Insanity." Sarah turned and holstered her smoking gun, the odor of burnt gunpowder wafting around her. Neither Ed nor the chief were going be too happy about this, but in her heart, she knew she had done the right thing.

She might be even able to prove Agnes and her cronies were involved, but somehow she doubted it. Maybe next Christmas she would have a few gifts of her own to dish out.

It was never too early to plan for next Christmas.

Robine's Diary

HAL TOMKINS SHIVERED as the damp sea breeze penetrated his thick navy pea coat sending chills through his flabby frame. He had once had a body reminiscent of a pro athlete, but that seemed like a lifetime ago, now he a sad ghost of his former self. It was on days like this he seemed older than any forty two year old should.

His nose wrinkled under the assault of the thick smell of rotting seaweed and dead fish that entered his mouth and nose with each ragged breath. His breathing was erratic from the exertion his having to climb over the lava rock.

The coal black jagged rocks littered the steep beach to the shoreline where he was headed.

Robine's Diary

Each step he took his feet ached due to the early onset of arthritis that was ravaging his body. An acute lack of exercise had made his five foot, seven inch frame swell, and his once wiry, vibrant red hair was now shot through with streaks of premature gray.

"I'm only forty-two, but I feel like I'm eighty," he murmured to himself under his breath.

His mouth was dry with a faintly metallic taste, the steel handle of his railway lantern held firmly in his right hand. He struggled his way across the jagged and slick boulders using what little light the lantern threw off to find his way in the inky darkness.

Balancing himself with the potato wedge-like fingers of his left hand on the tips of the larger boulders he carefully made his way toward his destination.

Fortunately, the lighthouse high above the beach filled the sky over him with its intense beam of white light that shot outward across the dark water, managed to bleed some additional light, but what little light there was cast eerie shadows over the black beach.

He was out here after dusk because he was certain he had seen something out of the ordinary near the waters edge. The burnt orange and red light at dusk had illuminated an unsettling shape he'd seen just before darkness chased away the last of the late fall day.

The moon wouldn't make its appearance for a couple of hours yet so he'd brought the lantern. He could have waited until then, or until morning, but he had to know what was down here. He wondered if one day his curiosity much like the proverbial cat would be the death of him. He wasn't afraid. He'd faced death down too many times to be afraid of it.

His heart beat hard in his chest as he stepped over another rock the lantern swinging to and for with each movement.

A sudden stiff breeze came up cutting through him like a rapier causing him to shiver in the damp air.

It's damn cold tonight.

Stopping to catch his breath the long unused muscles in his legs were on fire.

I'm an idiot to be out here.

Hal had been the lighthouse keeper on Merry Island for five years. In all that time he had never once missed his friends on the mainland or on Vancouver Island. Not that he didn't enjoy visitors. The crew of the monthly supply boat, for example, were a great couple of guys, but he valued his solitude more. Solitude to deal with his past.

The freighter's horn followed by the echo across the water made him look up from the rocks.

Robine's Diary

A massive vessel lit up like a Christmas tree, its deck piled high with steel containers, sat low in the water as it plowed through the sea about a mile from shore.

Forgetting to look down, Hal took a step, his boots slipped from underneath him and he landed hard on his bottom. His breath rushed from his lungs as a sharp pain shot up his spine. Gasping for air he managed a curse between grunts as he struggled to his knees. Sitting back on his haunches the heels of his boots resting against his sore bottom, he took in deep breaths of cold sea air as the pain gradually subsided.

"What am I doing out here?" he mused. "Com'on, old man you've been in worse spots than this."

Looking around he spotted the railway lantern lying on its side wedged between two rocks near the waters edge. It appeared to have survived the fall intact. the glow of its soft golden light the same as before. The light illuminated white topped waves that lapped against the shore.

Rising to his feet he started toward it when he suddenly froze. Peering into the gloom, Hal saw the light from the lantern had also illuminated something white sticking out of the sea. Small waves struck the object causing white foam to dance around it.

Fear crept up his throat as he recognized the shape as a human hand.

Hurrying toward the pale hand he stopped to pick up the lantern before coming to a halt at the shores edge. Holding the lamp out he saw the rest of the object attached to the hand hidden beneath the surface of the water.

Hal had once been in the army, having served with the peace keeping force in Rwanda, so the sight of a torn up human body was something he had seen before. What made this different was this someone he knew. her. No!

His breathing became strained and his body began to tremble. He dropped to his knees on the rocky beach. He placed his hands on his knees and took in great gulps of air as he struggled to keep down his dinner. Finally his mind stopped reeling, and his nostrils filled with the odor of the salty sweat dripping off his face. He managed to maintain his gaze at the woman beneath the water lying on her back with her unseeing eyes open.

It was definitely Jennifer Rohm.

The empty eye sockets, the long blond hair, the pink wetsuit with a white star over the left breast. Unmistakably it was her alright.

Only now half her face was missing, and an arm and a leg were gone, but there was no mistaking her, this body was Jennifer's. He had only met her last night when she and Miles —

Miles. Where was Miles Jacks?

His heart froze in his chest as a wave of grief and panic swept over him. They were such a lovely couple, both so bright and cheerful and full of life. Hal stopped and chastised himself. He barely knew these people. He'd only met then because yesterday when they had become separated from their charter group out of Secret Cove while sea kayaking.

Yesterday, Hal radioed the tour company to advise them Jennifer and Miles were safe at the lighthouse.

He recalled seeing them off this morning, friendly smiles all round and 'thanks you's' exchanged. Now she was dead. And Miles was missing.

Yesterday they were excellent dinner companions. The three of them talked like long lost friends well into the night about everything from politics to movies to the situation in the Middle East. As he recalled though, Miles was quite cryptic about his profession. He'd explained he was a consultant without any specifics.

In contrast, Jennifer spoke enthusiastically about her studies as a law student at the University of British Columbia.

Lovely, young, good-hearted, Jennifer Rohm was the epitome of the idealist law student. Jennifer Rohm was going to change the world.

Today someone had end her dreams forever

Hal moved closer to the lapping waves trying to decide if he should move her or leave her until he radioed the cops. They would want to check for evidence. He caught himself before he laughed.

Why am I thinking she died mysteriously? You read far too many crime novels, Hal old boy.

Her death must have been an accident. If he didn't pull her out then she might be pulled out with the tide. Then her family might never have a body to bury. Not knowing where your loved one was the worst of all nightmares for any family.

Finally, he decided and after placing the lamp carefully atop a nearby rock that had an almost perfect shelf carved into it by weather and wave action, he stepped into the water.

He wasn't about to take any chances on slipping and dropping the lamp a second time. He'd been lucky it hadn't smashed into a million pieces when he dropped it earlier.

Stepping carefully over the slick underwater rocks he was soon knee deep in the frigid water.

Robine's Diary

The cold sea water lapped near the tops of his boots. He shuddered when after he reached into the cold water his fingers made contact with the cold, bloated flesh of Jennifer's remaining arm.

He meant to drag her onto the shore. Glancing into the darkness behind and above him he realized the tide line extended some forty feet above the waters edge. Above the tide was green moss and dry yellow sea grasses. Somehow he would need to carry her up there or she'd again be washed out to sea with the high tide. The last tidal report he read said high tide would be at 5 a.m.. He had to get her out of here before then.

When she was whole, Jennifer probably only weighed ninety pounds, but he knew from experience dead bodies tended to be heavier, and were definitely more awkward to move, than carrying a conscious person. He corrected himself, a living person.

After considering his options he decided to heave her over his shoulders and carry her fireman style.

He soon had her out of the water releasing the smell of corpse. The stench mingled with the odor of the sea. A flood of memories invaded his thoughts. In his mind he saw acres of bloody human flesh stretching to the horizon, hacked apart like so much wheat with machetes wielded by crazed killers.

The images threatened to overwhelm him until he shook off those awful memories.

Sometimes he was thankful for the blackouts he occasionally suffered from since Rwanda. The military shrink had told him these would happen from time to time for a few years.

Planting his boots amongst the rocks he bent down and, after gripping her firmly around her torso, managed to lift her across his broad shoulders. She hung limply.

Moving carefully over the rocks, one step at a time, his breathing ragged in his ears, he carried her out of the water to the rocky shore. He paused to catch his breath and gather his strength for the climb up the rocks to the grass and moss.

He thought about retrieving the railway lamp, but decided against it because Jennifer's weight would shift if he bent down. He didn't want her to fall onto the rocks. Enough damage had been done to her.

After an agonizing climb, during which he thought his legs might give out at any moment, he finally arrived at the patch of dried grasses and soft moss. He dropped to his knees and let Jennifer's body slip off his shoulders to land with a soft thump and the whisper of the crush of dry grass.

With his lungs threatening to explode, Hal dropped face down in the soft moss breathing hard his nose filled with the pleasant scent of moss. He felt a sense of pride at accomplishing the climb up the hillside.

I'm so outta shape. His heart beat hard against his ribs and his breath came in ragged gulps. This is gonna kill me yet.

Rolling onto his back he threw his arms out from his sides. Opening his eyes he gazed at the dusting of stars overhead, twinkling brightly against the dark sky.

He tensed when he suddenly felt the presence of someone else standing above his head off to his left. He howled in protest and closed his eyes tightly as a swath of yellow light suddenly nearly blinded him.

"Who's there…what do ya think you're doin'?"

"Oh, thank God, Hal it's you."

"Who's there?" he said again

"Hal, it's me Miles…" The voice trailed off as the beam of light swung away to fall over Jennifer's body.

"Oh, my God! Jennifer!"

Hal heard the rush of footsteps over the grass coming from his right.

Hal opened his eyes to see spots dancing through his vision, but through the haze he made out Miles as he bent over Jennifer's torn body the flashlight beam focused on her shredded facial features. Hal shuddered.

Seeing her torn up the way she was reminded him of the horrors he'd seen in Rwanda. He'd come to this island to escape those terrible visions and yet here they were again.

Hal rolled to his stomach and with a grunt managed to get to his feet. Moving toward Miles who had one hand over his eyes while soft sobs wracking his lean, muscular frame.

Hal placed a hand on Miles shoulder. He felt the younger man flinch under his touch.

"What happened?" Miles said, his voice heavy with grief.

"Huh…I don't know, exactly. I suspect an accident. At least it looks like an accident." His heart went out the younger man. "I'm so sorry." Hal cringed at his inadequate words. Sorry never fixed anything.

Miles nodded. "What do we do now?"

"Well, I don't have standard operating procedures for such things, but I suggest we go to the house and radio the cops and the coast guard."

"I guess they'll investigate?"

Hal nodded. "Yeah. I suspect they will."

Why was Miles so interested in an investigation? Hal shrugged off the thought and helped Miles stand.

The younger man was shaky on his feet and as he swung the flashlight upward Hal could see dirty trails on his cheeks left by tears.

Hal led the way to the house. His home wasn't much really. Part office, part house it was a whitewashed single level stucco coated bungalow containing two bedrooms, a small kitchen, a bathroom, and a den.

Besides maintaining the lighthouse he was also required to provide daily weather reports to Environment Canada using a wind meter, a sensitive barometer and, most importantly his eyes.

There was a door that linked the house to the spiral staircase leading up to the powerful light in the twenty meter tall lighthouse. The beam of light it cast warned shipping to stay away from Merry Island or they'd be crushed against the rocks.

The rocky volcanic islands that dotted the inside passage between Vancouver Island and the mainland had created havoc in the early days of commercial shipping up and down the rugged west coast of North America since the days of the gold rush late in the 19th century.

Modern technology had made shipping very different.

Powerful diesel turbines propelled vessels longer than football fields. These monsters of the sea were piled high with steel containers, and equipped with sophisticated GPS satellite technology that would have been considered witchcraft by those nineteenth century sailing crews.

They arrived at the door to the house with Hal still gripping one of Miles arms. Jennifer's body had been left lying on the moss and grass where Hal intended to leave her untouched until the cops arrived. At first light he'd cover her with a tarp.

Hal opened to the door and stepped inside Miles came in behind him. The lights were still on so Hal blinked to clear his vision after being in the gloom outside.

Miles was dressed in blue jeans, gray and blue Addis, and a gray sweat shirt. Odd. Jennifer died wearing her wet suit. Why had Jennifer been alone? Miles told him last night kayakers always went out in teams. So why wasn't Miles also wearing a wetsuit? Hal shrugged. No doubt there was a simple explanation he hadn't considered.

Hal offered Miles a seat in an overstuffed chair in the living room while he called for help.

"I'll get the cops on the radio," he explained.

Robine's Diary

Not waiting for Miles response Hal hurried to the study where the door to the lighthouse stairs was. His lower back muscles shot agony up and down his back and legs with each step due to his earlier fall. He'd have a terrible bruise on his bottom by morning.

The door to the study was open so he stepped in and ran his hand over the light switch to turn the ceiling light on. Against one wall was a weathered roll top desk strewn with paperwork; tide reports, barometric and temperature, wind and wave reports that he was required to transmit by facsimile to the Environment Canada office in Vancouver each day. Next to the desk stood a six foot long by three foot wide pine table containing the fax machine and the shortwave radio.

Wheeling the captain's chair on its steel casters over the tiled floor to a spot in front of the table so he could use the short wave then he sat down. Pressing the on switch he was surprised when the dials didn't immediately light up. Bowing his head he looked underneath the table and saw the unit's power cable was intact and still plugged into the wall outlet.

Pulling the unit away from the wall he saw the problem. The rear access panel had been removed and the wires to the internal power supply had been cut.

Sabotage.

A trickle of cold sweat ran down his back. Who? Why? Was Jennifer's death involved somehow?

"What's going on?"

Hal started and swung round to find Miles was standing behind him, his dark eyes curious, and his expression flat. His dark curls were mashed flat and his pale skin was sallow. There were dark circles under his eyes. His thick black mustache needed trimming, tiny hairs sticking out in every direction like Hal's morning hair.

"Ummm…the radio is broken."

Hal stood still like a Michelangelo masterpiece as Miles leaned over the box and peered at the open panel and the cut wires. Hal watched as Miles' eyes narrowed and a frown creased his forehead. Hal's mouth felt like a dust bowl and his heart beat faster in his ears. Something was very wrong. Fear crept into him and he didn't know why.

"Did you cut the wires?" asked Miles, his words measured and deliberate. His eyes locked on Hal's, his expression bland.

Hal swallowed the last of his salvia and stepped away from the table and away from Miles.

"No, of course not. Did you?"

A slow sneer crossed Miles face and his eyes bore mild amusement. "Why would I do that?"

"Well…if you didn't and I didn't then who did?"

Hal shook his head. "I have no idea."

Miles looked thoughtful then said, "Then there has to be someone else on this island. And I think that someone killed Jenn."

Hal had said he thought it was an accident. Miles obviously thought otherwise. He must know something. Murder? Oh, no not again.

His mind reeled and the old feelings surfaced in him. The death. The blood. The awful memories threatened to overwhelm him.

A cold sweat broke out on Hal's arms, back, and legs. "I have to get out of here," he mumbled and his knees trembled. His bladder threatened to let loose any second.

Miles looked at his host a mildly curious expression on his face. "Why would you want get away? I mean there's two of us and one of him. We could catch a killer. We'd be heroes."

"You ever been one of them?" Hal asked, his voice trembling.

"What?"

"A hero."

Miles shrugged. "Nope. You?"

Hal's eyes flitted around the room which suddenly felt claustrophobic.

He whispered, "Yeah. When I was in the army. That's what they called us, heroes."

Miles looked curious. "Who, exactly?"

"The generals, the politicians, the newspapers, which we weren't...we stood by while..." His voice trailed off, the words caught in his throat as if by dry bread.

His heart beat faster in his chest, and he couldn't a breath as his chest tightened. Seeing his distress, Miles grabbed Hal by one of his arms and guided him to the captain's chair where he sat down heavily.

Leaning forward his elbows resting on his knees, Hal buried his face in his hands. His body shook violently as he was wracked by sobs. Until today he had never cried in front of anyone, not even the army shrink, or the chaplain. He was surprised how good it felt to share his pain, even with someone he had just met.

Finally, he regained in control and threw his head back in the chair, his eyes still closed. Fatigue clouded his mind as if he'd just completed a ten mile run with a full pack. Using the back of his hands he wiped the remaining tears from his cheeks and around his eyes. As his vision cleared he realized he was alone. Where was Miles?

He stood and moved to the doorway to the main room while calling Miles name. There was no response.

Moving into the main living area he heard a sound coming from his bedroom. It sounded like Miles was opening drawers as if he were searching for something. The guy had some nerve.

Entering the bedroom he found Miles had left every dresser drawer in the tall boy dresser open and had strewn Hal's clothes across the bedroom floor.

Miles was sitting on his unmade bed going through the contents of the one pine side table containing a lamp and radio alarm clock. The glowing red digits said it was eleven o'clock. Was it really that late?

"What're you doing?"

Miles continued to rummage through the drawer emptying to contents onto the floor. "What does it look like," he said, his back to Hal.

He pulled a second drawer out with enough force that the back of the drawer flew off. Emitting a snort of frustration, Miles threw the damaged drawer against the wall where it splintered and fell to the floor with a crash. Next he stood and, using both hands, he lifted the mattress off the box spring and shoved it hard off the other side of the bed.

Whirling to face him, Hal saw Miles eyes were flat, emotion free, and his breathing was normal even with the exertion of his search.

Cold bastard. Like I used to be.

Hal saw the muscles of Miles thick arms tighten beneath his shirt.

"What are you looking for?" Hal said his voice low, menacing.

"You will recall I'm sure I told you I was a consultant?" Hal nodded. "Well, in actuality I'm a gun for hire, a mercenary, and my employer wants something back —"

"What?" interrupted Hal, feeling a familiar anger in his belly he hadn't felt since seeing first the genocide wrought by the Hutu's and their allies when he was stationed with the United Nations Peace Keeping forces in Rwanda.

A sly smile crossed Miles features. "A diary. His daughter's diary. Apparently you brought it back with you from overseas…you know when…"

Hal had a sudden irresistible urge to wipe the smug smile off Miles face, but he knew he would have to wait for the right time. Miles could easily take him with one hand tied behind his back. He had to be smarter.

"I don't know what you're talking about."

Miles laughed. "Of course you do…Robine Gasana…surely you remember her…"

Hal felt his heart freeze in his chest. Yes, he did know her. Or rather he knew her, once. She was dead. She died in his arms, her throat cut, her warm blood running between his fingers. Since that dark time there was many a night he woke in a cold sweat still feeling her warm blood cascading over his hands as she died. She was only twenty years old. It was so unfair.

"Yes, I recall her," he whispered.

"She gave you a diary," said Miles matter-of-factly. "I want it." His voice was filled with menace.

"Or what? You'll murder me like you did Jennifer."

Miles snorted. "Don't be so dramatic, Hal." He shrugged and coldness came over Miles pale features reminiscent of the Rwandan killers of Hal's nightmares. Hal shivered at the recollection of those faces. "Besides, you killed Jennifer, not me."

Hal froze. He couldn't kill anyone after Rwanda. And certainly not Jennifer. How did Miles know? "You're lying. You're trying to confuse me."

Miles' eyes narrowed. "Believe what you want, but I know you killed her. I saw you, Hal." Miles shrugged. "Of course, you and I can make this go away, if —"

"If what?"

A small mirthless smile came over Miles lips. "Once you give me the diary I'll help you dispose of Jenn's body. If the cops find her they'll think she was cut up by the propellers of a passing freighter. Accidents happen you know. It's too bad really, she was a good gal." He sighed. "Oh well, easy come easy go."

Hal looked thoughtful as if he were seriously considering Miles offer. He needed time to formulate a plan. This smug bastard needed to be taught a lesson.

"What do we need to do?" he said at last.

Miles eased back until he rested against the edge of the desk, his arms he crossed over his chest. "Get me the diary." His dark gaze scanned the room as he spoke. "I tried to find it, but had no luck I'm afraid." His eyes locked on Hal's. "That's why I need you."

At that moment Hal knew if he gave Miles Robine's diary he was dead. In fact, he would have been dead already if Miles had managed to find it on his own.

Robine. A name he would never forget. He still saw her gentle features in his dreams. Her dusky, smooth complexion, her full lips, her high cheeks bones, eyes the color of inky pools of cool water....

"It's in the lighthouse, at the top where the light is...outside on the deck..."

Miles nodded. "Well then, let's get a move on. You lead the way."

Hal nodded and led the way through the door to the lighthouse from his office. They were quickly up the steel spiral staircase and through the hatch into the heart of the lighthouse. The high intensity light flashed outward to warn passing vessels of the rocks far below.

"Don't look at the light," warned Hal as Miles came through the hatch.

At the rear of the chamber was a small door just large enough for one full sized man to get through. It led to the narrow railed deck outside. It ran completely around the outside of the light chamber.

"Out there," Hal yelled over the sound of the generator that powered the motor that made the light revolve. He nodded in the direction of the door. Miles frowned looking uncertain.

Hal headed for the small door, ducking low to make it through. He was quickly outside in the darkness. The wind was stronger out here than on the beach forcing him to have to lean into the stiff breeze.

Hal stood to one side of the steel door as Miles put one leg out. As Miles torso began to appear Hal stepped forward and, using his full body weight, he body slammed the door as hard as he was able into Miles.

Miles cried out in pain then his leg slid back inside the chamber and Hal heard him hit the floor.

Hal's breathing came hard and his heart pounded in his ears from the sudden rush of adrenaline. Pulling the door back he stepped inside and saw Miles face. The door had caused a deep gash on his forehead that was bleeding profusely spilling blood down his shirt and into his eyes. The chamber's air was filled with the all too familiar iron smell of blood making him gag. Closing his eyes Hal willed the nausea away.

After opening his eyes, he gazed at the still form of Miles lying on his back on the floor. His chest was rising and falling in rhythmic breathing. Good, he's alive.

All he needed to do was carry him out of here. He'd lock him in here until he could reach the cops.

But he'll tell the cops I killed Jennifer which I didn't. What do I do?

Reaching down, Hal grasped Miles hands in his and dragged the unconscious man out the small door onto the deck. He was laying face down so Hal rolled him onto his back. Miles arms flopped to his sides as if he were a rag doll.

Hal stared into the face of the man who only moments ago meant to murder him like he had Jennifer. His heart froze and the old coolness from his days in the army flooded his brain exorcising any trace of humanity.

Wiping his mouth with the back of his hand, he stood and started for the door.

His eyes narrowed. The coldness of the warrior he'd been so well schooled in during his army days enveloped him. Hal had no compassion for the man. Miles was a killer. A hired gun to do someone else's dirty work.

Suddenly, thick strong fingers grabbed his left ankle in a vice like grip. Looking down he saw Miles was awake blood dripping in rivulets down his face from his head wound. Hal's heart beat hard and he pulled his leg to try and loosen the enraged man's grip. But Miles fingers gripped him tightly, desperately, his face twisted in rage.

Miles was stronger than him. Suddenly Hal lost his footing and fell backwards to land in a heap on top of the now conscious man. Miles body bucked beneath him like a pro wrestler causing Hal to roll onto his side. His face now pressed hard against the cold steel railing.

He grunted as he felt increasing pressure from behind him pressing him harder into the steel bars. Realizing he would black out soon he knew he had to do something now, or it was all over.

Trying to reach behind him to relief the increasing pressure Hal couldn't get a grip on anything.

"You're gonna die, solider boy," he heard Miles growl. "The Hutu shoulda killed you all in Rwanda. You bastards did nothing to stop the slaughter."

Hal felt something deep from somewhere inside him suddenly snap. Anger surged over him like as tidal wave. We did what we could! The world failed the Tsui's not me!

With a wild yell and snarl Hal pressed back hard against the pressure on his back and felt it give way. Roaring he jumped to his feet and faced Miles who had also scrambled to his feet.

His tormentor was blinking the blood from his eyes, his face twisted in a snarl. Hal stepped up and threw a round house punch at Miles head. Miles was still fast as he side stepped the punch and elbowed Hal in the side of his head as he stepped forward.

Hal's heart rate increased as adrenaline coursed through his veins. No! He's not beating me! He was trained to kill. The army had trained him well. It was time to shake off the rust and take care of business.

Shaking off the blow with a grunt he spun and threw a kick that hit Miles hard in the center of his chest. The kick was of sufficient force that it lifted Miles off his feet. His face registered his surprise then he was gone over the railing and into the darkness.

Robine's Diary

A terrified scream erupted which was quickly lost on the wind.

Trembling, his knees buckling, Hal sank to the steel deck, gasping for breath, his arthritic knees sending shock waves of pain up his legs. Squinting he peered over the railing into the darkness below him. There was no sign of Miles.

Gritting his teeth, Hal managed to pull himself up and stand just as the new moon appeared in the sky to cast its soft glow over the island. It was then, as he looked down he saw Miles broken body lying on the rocky shore far below. His calm returned, the bloodlust quickly waning. His shoulders sagged as grief enveloped him and his humanity returned.

With cold salty tears streaming down his face, Hal turned and stumbled toward an access panel only he and the original builders of the lighthouse knew about. Loosening the screws he removed the cover and reached inside. Relief washed over him as he felt the plastic cover. Grasping the object in his fingers he pulled Robine's diary from its hiding place.

Sliding down the cement wall of the lighthouse he landed on his bottom on the deck once again. Hal hugged the precious diary to his chest. Robine's diary was the only record that his Tutsi wife ever existed.

It contained detailed accounts of the massacre, naming names. Powerful names of people that would pay anything and kill anyone to hide their heinous crimes from the world.

Tears flowed down his cheeks. He began to sob. Robine must be avenged. Those responsible must pay. It was time. Time to release her diary and the truth to the world.

Loose Ends

S HIT!"
Dan Fargas hopped on his left foot
gripping his injured right in two meaty hands. His
mouth spat a string of expletives in his vain attempt
ease the pain. His normally pale face was as red as
Rudolf's nose.

Sheila Willis, the senior investigator on the
Vancouver Homicide squad, and Dan's superior officer,
wore a look of disgust on her tanned, narrow face as
she stood watching her younger partner. The guy was
a living loose end she'd been saddled with by the boss.
She detested loose ends.

She shook her head, her long thin arms crossed
over her smallish bosom. Her right foot tapped out her
impatience with the bumbling rookie.

Loose Ends

The superintendent had saddled her with him two months ago. It wasn't the pain in his foot that bothered her as much as the pain in the ass the guy had turned out to be.

"Fargas watch where you're walking," she said keeping her voice low so as not to alert the uni's inside that her partner was such a fumble foot. He'd stubbed his toe on the cement steps leading to the front door of the house at 1422 Maple.

Sheila sighed inwardly. There were only three steps for God's sake. Surely he could manage three steps? "I guess not," she said to herself under her breath.

Fargas looked at her quizzically. "What?" He eased his injured foot to the ground and winced.

"Never mind fumble foot let's go."

She started up the stairs holding the yellow police line tape up for her hobbled partner to duck underneath as they reached the open door. The peeled paint left on the weathered door suggested it used to be sky blue. From what she'd seen the house was the typical bungalow for the neighborhood. Sheila paused before entering to slip into the skin-tight white surgical gloves she wore on her belt. Once she had on the gloves she pulled her notebook from the inside pocket of her black leather jacket.

Triple homicide, the on site uni's had reported, which was why they were here. She was certain this was gonna get messy — fast.

She nodded grimly at Fargas who had also donned his gloves, and had his own notebook in his right hand. At least he was following procedure <u>this time</u>.

He nearly blew the Harper case out of the water when his prints were found all over the kitchen. Imagine raiding a victim's fridge while investigating their murder? Fuckin' dumb ass. That Justice guy who covered up Dan's slop was good no doubt about it.

She entered to find two uniforms standing over the body of a young Chinese woman. She'd been shot in the center of her forehead. Very little blood on the floor, but the wall behind her was sprayed with blood and brains. The air in here was warm and smelled of cooked fish.

The female uni grunted as she glanced up to see Sheila and Fargas enter. "Hey, Sarge how's it hanging, eh?"

Sheila knew this constable. Dicks was it? Yup, there was her nametag R Dicks. "Not bad, Dicks. You?"

Dicks was a woman barely twenty-five, with a face that bore the evidence of too many bloody crime scenes.

She shrugged her broad shoulders then looked back down at her notebook as she wrote. Sheila concluded the bun of blond hair atop her hatless head was wound too tight.

"Okay," said Dicks.

Sheila walked up and knelt down next to the body. "Anyone taken the pics yet?" She glanced up from her notebook at Dicks.

Dicks shook her head. "Naw. The wagon with the coroner is on its way." She paused and lifted her right arm to look at her watch then wrote the time in her notebook. Sheila did the same in hers. "Should be here any minute."

"Any ident yet?"

Dicks shook her head never taking her gray eyes off her notebook. "Nope. No wallets. No purses. Nothing. Odd don't ya think?"

"Yeah. Odd." Good, thought Sheila.

"We got other bodies?" said Sheila glancing around the room. It was a very average living room for average people. Ordinary really. Difference between the ordinary and not so ordinary was average people don't get shot in their average living rooms.

White walls with those K-Mart knock off art pictures of trees on them.

A large potted palm in one corner with a small TV on a wire stand under the large front picture window that faced the street. She made a mental note of that fact. The house faced south so the afternoon sun would make watching the TV difficult, if not impossible. Particularly in the summer when the days were longer.

There was a large three-person brown corduroy covered couch against the far wall facing the TV. The forest green carpet that covered the floor was one of those cheap indoor-outdoor types. The kind you could buy at any one of those discount carpet places in Richmond. Not much in the room for a place that people lived in. No books, magazines or ornaments adorned the two rough oak end tables on either side of the couch. Though there were two pale pink porcelain coffee table lamps, one on each end table.

Sheila smirked. No accounting for taste, bad or otherwise.

While it was early in the investigation yet she thought the place might be seen as a grow op. Maybe they'd find the basement stuffed with fragrant pot plants up to the rafters. The couch and the TV placement might be for the lookouts entertainment while they watched for rival gangs or cops.

Yeah, might be. She filed the thought mentally for a later time.

Of course, these days perps weren't too worried about cops raiding grow ops. Judges and their lenient sentencing had made the cops shift resources to other more pressing duties. Busting a grow op cost way too much in time and money when the perps often walked away with a small fine. Rival gangs on the other hand, they had no get-out-of-jail-free card. She filed this observation too away for future reference.

"Yeah." Dicks nodded at her male partner who wore with a thin smile on his dusky features. "Phil will show you." He was a strapping black man with pure white teeth and a twinkle behind those dark expressive eyes.

Sheila held out her right hand and returned the smile. "Phil…?"

The male uni chuckled lightly as he took her hand in his and shook it. "Yeah. Philip J. Rasmussen at your service."

His handshake was firm and my, wasn't he the little charmer? Good looks, and good manners. What a welcome relief from some of the disastrous dates her girlfriend, Connie had insisted she go on in the past year. Divorced cops just weren't good cougar material.

Hold on, Sheila, she reminded herself. We're working, Willis. Now's not the time for romance.

"Well then, Phil why don't you lead the way?"

Rasmussen nodded then led the two detectives down a short hallway to the back bedroom. There was only one bedroom. This wasn't uncommon for these old wartime houses.

As they entered the room it was clear the carnage was far more in here. The walls were sprayed bloody and the bed contained two lumps of torn red flesh lying side by side. They must've been naked at the time of the shootings because they didn't appear to be wearing any clothing. Definitely a man and a woman. Another Chinese woman by the look of her. The guy was white.

The only way she could tell actually was by the flesh visible on the areas of the corpses not covered by blood. The faces had been mutilated and in the areas where most human genitalia were located were two black holes. The perp had shot them both in the privates with what was obviously a larger caliber weapon.

The room was permeated by iron blood and rotting flesh. Flies danced over the corpses hovering like greedy calves at their mother's tit. We're all ultimately worm food, thought Sheila with a smirk.

Someone really didn't like these people. The question now was if the shot to the genital area was post-mortem. She suspected the shots to their heads were the killing blows, but she expected the medical examiner would be able to tell her for certain.

From behind her she heard the sound of someone retching. She glanced over her shoulder to see Fargas covering his mouth with both hands and looking all the world like the worst case of the flu in history. His short blond hair was matted with a sudden flood of sweat.

"Fuck," he breathed before he disappeared down the hall and out the front door.

She glanced at Rasmussen who smiled and shrugged his broad shoulders. She rolled her eyes then went back to studying the murder scene.

This was definitely murder, and from the look of it there was an element of revenge. No, this wasn't what she thought might be the link that tied these murders at first. No, no gang involvement this was personal. Too bad, she had hoped to add this one to the many unsolved gang slayings on the books.

This room wasn't going to tell her much more. Forensics would hopefully tell her the details she needed. Hopefully these three's fingerprints would be on file with the RCMP lab in Ottawa, but she doubted it. She wasn't having a good Christmas so far. She knew she'd need a break and a bit of luck if she were going to solve this one before Mother's Day.

"He a Christmas present from the inspector?" said Rasmussen, indicating the empty doorway where Fargas had disappeared.

Sheila grimaced. "Yeah. But not the one I asked the head Christmas elf for I assure you."

Rasmussen smirked. "Know what you mean, Sarge."

Sheila went back down the hallway until she was standing again in the living room next to the young woman's body. The dead eyes were still staring at the ceiling.

"One more question, Dicks then I gotta go," said Sheila stopping beside Dicks who was still making notes. At times like this Sheila was glad not be on patrol anymore.

"Yeah." Impatience crept into Dicks tone. Sheila felt mild irritation at Dick's attitude, but decided she didn't want to die on this hill so she let it slide.

"I know this isn't likely, but by any chance do we have a murder weapon?"

Dicks smirk told her what she needed to know even before she spoke. "Nope. Sorry."

They heard the squeak of brakes outside as Fargas walked into the room his face a blanket of snow, his blood shot eyes swollen. "The coroner's here," he said.

Sheila ignored the little piss-ant. "Thanks, Dicks didn't think so. I'm not gonna snag a present here am I?"

Dicks shrugged and headed out to greet the coroner. Sheila followed her and signaled with a sweep of her left hand for Fargas to follow. For his part he appeared properly cowed. He looked at the floor as they went outside, her in the lead.

The coroner for Vancouver was a young man about thirty five-ish. His predecessor has just been elected mayor so this guy was the new man. Sheila was told he came highly recommended. Before accepting the city's offer he'd been assistant coroner in Toronto for five years so he probably knew his stuff.

When Sheila arrived beside the black Chevy sedan, Tom Par was removing what looked a lot like a navy blue fishing tackle box from the trunk as Dicks was briefing him on what to expect once inside. Dicks' looked up from her notebook just as Sheila and Fargas arrived.

"The detectives are here, Mr. Par. Rasmussen and I will stay on scene to keep away press and curious neighbors."

"Thank you, constable." Par held out his right hand, which she took in hers.

He was a weasel of a man with wire rimmed glasses and mouse brown hair that looked as if it had been cut by it's owner. The ends were jagged and strands seemed to stick out in every direction.

He was medium height, slim and his beady hazel eyes squinted back at her. His voice was reedy and would be annoying if you were forced to listen to it too long.

"Detective." Par nodded. "I assume you want a photo layout and cause of death asap?"

Good the guy got down to business right away. She was beginning to like the new man already and she'd only just met him. "Yes, sir. That would be very much appreciated if I'm gonna get him — the killer I mean."

"How do we know the killers a man?" said Par, his eyebrows arched.

Sheila smirked and put her hands in the pockets of her leather jacket. Her nine-millimeter suddenly felt heavy in her shoulder holster. "We don't, of course. But in my experience I've very rarely seen a woman resort to this level of violence."

Par nodded. "Yeah. Dicks here filled me in. In the genitals, huh? Nope, I've never seen a case like that before. Should be quite the challenge." He slipped on his rubber surgical gloves with a snap.

Sheila looked at him and nodded. She pulled out her wallet and retrieved two of her business cards. "Here, sir is my card. Call me on my cell day or night. I really want to nail this guy."

"Okay," said Par with a shrug of his narrow shoulders as he lifted his tackle box and started for the steps to the front door.

"Here, Dicks take the other card and give it to Phil. Ask him to call me later."

"I ain't no cupid," said Dicks looking dubious.

"Yeah, I know, but do it anyway. Okay?"

Dicks nodded and stuffed the card in the front pocket of her bulletproof vest that covered her navy police shirt. When she was a uni Sheila always hated wearing those damn things. Too hot. Made you sweat like you were in the Sahara even when the temperature outside was near zero.

"We're goin'. You think of anything else call me. Okay?"

Dicks nodded then turned and headed for the house. Phil stood on the front stoop waiting for his partner. He threw Sheila a brief smile as she turned and headed for her gray unmarked Chevy sedan. Fargas followed her like a lost puppy.

Once they were on the road headed in the direction of the station on Main Street Sheila made a decision. "Ya know, Dan, I have a thought."

Fargas looked at her with puzzlement written all over his boyish face. "Yeah?"

"I think we should go down to the Angels club house on Powell and have a chat with the boys. Maybe they'll know these people. What do you think?"

Fargas shrugged. "If you think so, Sarge, but I don't see how they would be able to help us. In fact, I don't see any connection to the bikers so far at all."

Sheila smiled. "Now that's the first time you didn't try to kiss my ass. I'll make a real walking, talking detective outta you yet, Fargas. You know how I hate loose ends." Sheila slapped the steering wheel of the Chevy. "Fuck it! Let's go for a drive in the park. Call it my Christmas present to you."

Fargas' cheeks turned red and he looked properly humiliated. Good. That'll teach the young know-it-all not to barf around her crime scenes.

She gunned the engine and weaved her way through the light Christmas day traffic until they reach the entrance to Lord Stanley's Park. She slowed as they entered the park. The brightly decorated harbor was visible off to their right as they drove. A breeze had sprung up and the surface of the bay that normally was an unbroken blanket pale gray was dotted with light white caps.

They drove along the road next to the harbor in silence until they came to the bypass road after Brockton

Point with its colorfully carved native canoe pointing the way to the Lion's Gate Bridge that connected Vancouver proper with North and West Van. The bridge was decorated with multicolored Christmas lights making the sixty year-old plus suspension bridge appear bright and cheery.

Sheila felt cold inside. She didn't relish what she had to do, but the young cop next to her would be trouble later. He may be a fumble foot rookie but he wasn't stupid. He'd never have made detective at his age if he didn't have the smarts.

She pulled over and parked by the side of the road. There was a footpath leading into the woods. The forest was green and cool and she could smell the pine and oak in the air as she stepped from the car. She took in a deep breath. The crisp air felt good after the haze of blood smells at the house they'd just left.

"Why are we here?" said Fargas who'd exited the car and stood with his hands in the pockets of his brown suede jacket. He shifted his feet as he stood causing him to sway. He looked around his breath leaving a trial of wispy mist in the cool air.

Sheila moved to the back of the car and popped the trunk lid. She pulled out a plastic Safeway shopping bag then slammed the trunk close again.

"Follow me," she said and started down the pathway. Fargas shrugged and followed her keeping his hands buried in his pockets.

After a short hike they reached a clearing where Sheila stopped and stood while Fargas moved around casually studying the tall fir and pine trees that surrounded the clearing, he looked puzzled.

Sheila drew a Saturday night special she'd strapped to her leg near her ankle and thumbed the safety to the off position. Fargas' eyes went wide. "What the fuck are you doing?" His face paled.

"I'm going to kill you, Fargas," she said simply her dark eyes as cold as the winter air.

"But damn it, it's Christmas!" said Fargas his voice edged with desperation. He looked around for any possible escape route. As he did so he reached inside his jacket to retrieve his own gun. It was a desperate move that he didn't finish before a shot rang out in the silent forest.

A look of surprise registered on Fargas' face as he looked down at his chest where there was now a small dark hole in his pale green shirt. A splotch of blood appeared and began to spread like a stone thrown into a still pond. His eyes suddenly rolled up in his head and he dropped face down onto the forest floor like a puppet whose strings had abruptly been cut.

Loose Ends

"Merry Christmas," breathed Sheila, the barrel of her gun trailing a small puff of white smoke. This was the second time she'd fired the weapon in the past 24 hours. The shotgun in the trunk of the Chevy had even more of a workout when she shot that bitch and her ex in the bedroom. She was glad Bill and those two whores were dead.

The butt of her off duty gun was wrapped in duct tape, and she'd filed the serial numbers off after she bought it off Garcia two years previous. It was unlikely that even if it were found they'd be able to link her to the gun.

She gazed at Dan's body lying still on the forest floor and felt an odd sense of satisfaction. He'd be reported missing tomorrow though his body would be badly decomposed before, or even if he was found. She'd naturally feign no knowledge of his whereabouts. Who'd suspect a homicide detective? She'd probably be in charge of the case. Another unsolved murder for the books.

She smiled inwardly sometimes you need to just go out and get what you really want for Christmas for yourself even if you had to kill to get it.

She opened the shopping bag and first pulled out a steel garden spade.

Then she slipped on another pair of surgical gloves and moved to the edge of the forest where she began to dig a hole in the soft rich soil.

After the hole was deep enough she placed the remainder of the contents of the bag, two ladies handbags, and man's wallet, along with her off duty piece and the spade in the hole. Then with her gloved hands she pushed the dirt back into the hole covering everything. She smoothed the dirt until it was flat then covered it with leaves and other forest refuse. She was satisfied when the area looked as undisturbed as the rest of the forest floor.

Nope, no one will find this stuff. She smirked as she stood and brushed the rich earth off the knees of her black jeans..

She paused to cast one last glance at her late partner. One loose end all tied up with ribbon. "Happy New Year," she murmured then turned and walked away.

From cover of the bushes near the edge of the clearing a pair of muddy eyes watched Sheila disappear from view.

It Takes Two

"WHAT'S THE NAME?" Frank Upton said his attention focused on the worn leather notebook he'd pulled from his K-Mart suit pocket. He stood on the narrow urban street outside the smoldering ruin of the house on Church Street where the charred — and as yet unidentified — remains had been found.

Sergeant Hal Folsom, his partner of ten years, was the first officer on the scene after the Fire Department investigator found the body and made the call for police presence.

"The FD's Peterson is on this one," Folsom said, his well chewed gum snapping between his perfectly straight white teeth.

Folsom worked out more than Frank, consequently he wore the better suits from one of those upscale places at the mall. His blond crew cut and muscular build made the single detective popular with all the gals at the station house and some of the guys too. Rumor was his folks left him a big bankroll which certainly didn't hurt his social life.

He was known as a real swordsman around the precinct. There were persistent rumors he'd even bagged a few of the married lady cops, but since he wasn't one to kiss and tell, the rumors were unconfirmed. Frank wasn't about to ask his younger partner since he had little interest in how another man took his lovin'.

Frank scratched the side of his head where the fringe of his remaining dark brown hair stuck out from beneath the edge of his wide brimmed fedora. He'd never been much for fashion, but he was pleased when hats came back into style. Of course, this meant he was ribbed incessantly by his fellow cops. He knew that behind his back they called him Frank Spade, junior G-Man. But this didn't bother him. He liked the look and it did hide his balding dome.

"Okay, Gus (Frank nicknamed the younger man Gus due to his mule like attitude when he'd been a rookie detective.

The name, which stemmed from an old movie he'd seen when his kids were small, stuck) we'll get the vics name from the ME."

He turned away and studied the smoking pile of wood framing all that remained of the once multistory, old house. At the rear of the blackened skeleton stood an immense stone chimney that must've reached up to the roof four stories up. The top half collapsed as the walls caved in.

The house was one of the old style with the extended wooden porch in front where Moms and Dads would sit in rocking chairs for hours watching their children play on the street in front. An old fashioned kind of place with a tall old oak sitting majestically near a sagging white picket fence dotted with peeling paint. Some of the pickets were absent, reminding Frank of a Halloween pumpkin with missing teeth.

The grass, burned black near the foundation of the old house, was over grown near the fence obviously long neglected by its owner.

"Anyone else here when this happened?" asked Frank, his dark eyes narrowed as he studied the remains of the building. Frank believed the clues to every murder were right in front of you all the time, all you had to do was find them.

Hal shook his head. "Nope. The neighbor across the street --" Hal paused to flip back a page in his notebook. Unlike Frank's, Hal's notebook was polished black leather -"Mrs. Wallace called 911 at 2030 hours – she said the entire place was engulfed in flame – the FD guys said they got here in time to make sure the flames didn't jump to the next house and take down anymore of these relics—"

Frank glanced both ways. Gus was right there were a lot of these old houses on this street. Fire traps every one of them. He shook his head. This one going up as quick as it did was probably a blessing in disguise. Maybe now some of these old farts would get the message to dump these places and move into one of those senior buildings out by route three. After, some smart builder with a lot of capital would clean up building a string of cheap condos on this land.

"Did Peterson say why he called us?"

"Yeah. He said the center of the fire was a light bulb in the study where the body was found. He found evidence of an accelerant. Probably gasoline."

Frank nodded. "Okay. Let's wrap this up here. Make sure the criminalist gets some good photos. You and I will talk to the ME in the morning."

Frank left Gus to wrap up the neighbor interviews and headed home to his one bedroom apartment on Front Street in his blue eighty seven Chevy. The car was his pride and joy, it was the one thing Sharon left him in divorce settlement and he babied the damn thing.

***

At exactly the stroke of nine thirty the next morning — he liked to sleep late — Frank drove his car into the parking lot of the station to find Hal standing leaning on his own car, a cherry red Mustang, with his arms crossed over his wide chest waiting for him. His wry smile and knowing gaze meant he'd found something. He was working on a piece of gum just as he did every day, all day. Frank wondered if the guy owned shares in a chewing gum company.

He turned off the engine and the heavy door squeaked slightly as he opened it to step out. He frowned. Where the hell had that come from? He held the door open with one hand and stepped around the side to study the hinges. Willie at the garage should have oiled the hinges last month. He needed to…

"Hey, Frank," said Hal as he approached with his hands buried in the pockets of his chinos his black leather jacket open, flapping around him.

His polished gold badge attached to his belt gleamed in the bright sunlight.

Frank stood; a frown fixed to his ruddy complexion, and slammed the car door hard. Hal's handsome features broke into a smile. "Car trouble?"

"Yeah," said Frank sullenly. He turned to study Hal with a suspicious look. "What the fuck are you doin' out here?"

"I wanted to be the first to tell ya," said Hal a big grin wedded to his face. "Ya know, before the cap'n gives me a medal or sumthin'".

"Gus, what are you babbling about?" Frank stood straight and eyed his partner. He smoothed his long gray rain coat and pushed his gray fedora, the one with the black band, back on his head, his hands now in his pockets. Frank thought he smelled a rat.

"I solved the case of the burnt house," said Hal with obvious pride.

Frank pulled his hands out of his pockets and crossed his arms over his narrow chest. Hal had this annoying habit of naming their cases, like he was Sherlock freaking Holmes. "Listen, Gus..."

"No, Frank, you can't call me that anymore. I'm not a rookie anymore, no siree. No, Frank. I've been your partner for five years, and for five years you've called me that name and I'm sick of it.

My name is Hal and I solved the case without you. I think that deserves some credit, don't you?"

Frank gapped at the younger man, his mouth open. He closed his mouth and thought carefully before speaking. Maybe Gus — no Hal, he corrected himself is right. Let's hear what he's got to say, then decide.

Frank shrugged. "Okay, Hal, why don't you fill me in."

As they walked into the police stations hundred year old red brick building Hal explained. The victims wife Emily Butters, the deceases name was apparently Percival Butters, a famous short story writer (who Frank never heard of until this minute) appeared early this morning at the station in response to a call for witnesses to come forward. The request for information was broadcast by the police department's media relations department.

When Mrs. Butters met with Hal this morning, after only a few questions, she confessed to killing her husband of seventy-five years. The victim, Mr. Butters, was ninety years of age.

Frank and Hal arrived outside the interrogation room.

It Tales Two

On the other side of the one way glass sat an old woman with shoulder length white hair and gnarled hands with a white Styrofoam cup of steaming tea (there was a string from a teabag dangling over side of the cup) in front of her. She wore a faded pastel white, yellow and red dress that covered her withered form from neck to knees, and a beige knitted shawl rested across her humped shoulders. Her eyes studied the room as if she were casing the layout. The gentle features of her pale wrinkled face was fixed in a small smile.

Interesting woman, Frank thought.

Propped against the plain, smooth blue steel table was a brown wooden cane, the ornately carved gleaming brass handle, in the shape of a dragon's head stopped it from falling over.

Frank frowned as he watched the old woman pick up her tea, take a sip then place it back on the table. Her hand didn't tremble, something common to older people. The cane might be her way of making people think she was infirm. Tea and sympathy was the worlds oldest scam.

He scratched the stubble on his chin and straightened his narrow dark tie. He'd not bothered to close the top button of his wrinkled pale green shirt so he did so now. He signaled to Hal to wait out here.

Hal scowled and crossed his arms across his wide chest.

Frank moved to the door and, after pasting a hopefully friendly grin on his face, went inside the room. Mrs. Butters smiled warmly as he walked through the door. She watched him cross the room and sit opposite her in the steel framed gray chair.

He folded his hands with his arms resting on the table. "Hello, Mrs. Butters, I'm Detective Frank Upton —"

"Do you work with that nice young man?" she said her voice as gentle as his own grandmother. God rest her soul.

"Huh…yeah…"

"Good. He's a very polite young man. So nice to see that the younger generation has such nice manners —" Frank had to regain control of the interview so he interrupted her.

"Mrs. Butters, please." Mrs. Butters stopped and smiled sweetly her arms folded in her lap, her expression calm waiting for him to continue.

Frank studied her weathered features then continued. "Mrs. Butters, I hope you realize that you've confessed to a very serious crime. And quite honestly you don't look the type." Frank pulled his handkerchief from his back pocket and used it to wipe down his neck.

It was warm in the room; the air conditioning was on the fritz again. He caught a whiff of his perspiration already forming under his arm pits. Damn, I hate the heat.

"Yes, it's certainly warm isn't it detective?" said Mrs. Butters keeping her shawl about her shoulders. "I just don't feel it like I used to."

He nodded. "So, Mrs. Butters, why don't you tell me what happened? From the beginning." Mrs. Butters nodded and smiled

"He wouldn't write what I like," she said smugly.

"Pardon?"

"Percy, is such a damned snob. He writes literary fiction. I love the old fashioned mystery stories."

"Huh, I don't follow…" said Frank.

Emily Butters looked up at the ceiling and rolled her eyes, clearly exasperated at his lack of understanding. "It's a wonder you people solve any crimes at all," she muttered. Frank started to protest when she held up her right hand to stop him.

"I've been asking Percy to write a mystery story for me for fifty years, and for fifty years he's refused. He said his public demanded more high-brow fiction, and genre fiction is only for profit. Can you imagine? Heaven help us if his writing actually made us some money." She rolled her eyes and snorted.

"So you killed him?"

"Yes," she said with conviction.

"Because he wouldn't write a mystery?"

"Yes. And the final straw, of course."

Frank thought this interrogation was like pulling hairs off a sows butt. He made a circular motioned with his hand for her to continue. She smiled thinly and said, "His self proclaimed biggest fan sent him a gift with a note saying he was the most brilliant writer of all time. He showed it to me and said he'd never write me a mystery now. That's when I added the poison to his pen."

Frank was startled by this bit of information. According to the FD's report the blaze that killed Mr. Butters started at the desk lamp, once the gasoline in the light bulb ignited the fire consumed him and the room within seconds. It was rigged to explode. Now a poisoned pen? The lady was certainly poetic if nothing else.

"Poison pen?"

"Yes. Percy was an old fashioned man who had used ink wells when he was a boy, even though these days he uses a ball point pen. Old habits die hard, he would dab the tip of the pen on the tip of his tongue to wet it in between sentences.

I added digitalis to the ink in the ball point pen and sat back to wait for him to have a heart attack or stroke. The fire, probably caused by him dropping his lit pipe, must've been after his heart attack. So I killed him."

Frank scratched his head in thought. What was he going to tell her?

Hal burst through the door interrupting them. "Frank, we need to talk." His wide eyes and pale face told Frank that something was definitely wrong.

Frank smiled easily at Mrs. Butters. "Why don't we go into my office and have a seat? You'll be more comfortable there. Detective Folsom and I have to check something, okay?"

Mrs. Butters nodded and the three went into the squad room where they left Mrs. Butters sitting in the padded chair next to Frank's desk. They went into the Captain's office where the chief of detectives, Captain Neal Reilly, sat behind his plain brown desk gazing at them, a frown wrinkling his dusky forehead. His dark eyes bored into the two detectives as they sat in the two green padded metal office chairs across from him.

"You better have a good explanation," said Reilly in his deep voice. His corpulent body, encased in white shirt and dark red power tie, made him an imposing figure.

He eased back in his high backed leather office chair and wiped his dark brow with a white handkerchief. The room reeked of his sour perspiration.

Frank glanced inquiringly at Hal. "Cap'n, Frank has a woman in interview two who says she killed Percy Butters too," explained Hal. His cheeks were flushed because he'd told Captain Reilly he had a confession already in this case.

Frank's eyes went wide and he sat back against the chairs thin cushion even though he knew his shirt would stick to the vinyl surface.

"And who's this second killer?" said Frank after several seconds of silence.

"She says she's Percival Butters biggest fan," said Reilly his voice at the same time somber and irritated. Frank wondered how he managed to do that. Guess that's why he's the boss.

"Well, I'll be…" breathed Frank.

"What?" said Reilly. He was a stern cop but a good one. He didn't like complications or surprises when it came to murder investigations. He'd been pleased when the Butters case had been so easily closed. Now it had become overly complicated.

"Mrs. Butters just told me Mr. Butters received a gift in the mail…from his biggest fan…"

"Let me guess, the gift was a light bulb," said Hal sardonically.

Frank shook his head. "I don't know…she didn't say…but that would make sense." He frowned. "Maybe one of those full spectrum lights."

Reilly leaned forward his fingers interlaced and rested his elbows on his desk. He glared at the two men. "You better find out and fast. I don't want these two getting lawyered up and make this mess into a total legal shambles."

Frank and Hal nodded in unison and they left the Captain's office. As they made their way back to Frank's desk Hal leaned toward him and whispered, "Sorry about earlier. I think you better talk to the lady in two. Alone."

Frank's eyes narrowed at he gazed at his young partner. Coward. "Yeah, okay. What's the name?"

"Roberta Sommers."

They stopped beside Frank's desk where Mrs. Butters sat reading a magazine someone had given her. It was the latest issue of the Police Gazette.

She shook her head in wonderment as they approached. "My, you boys are busy aren't you?"

"Yes, ma'am," said Frank with a slight grin. "Detective Folsom is going to stay with you and record your statement. I'll be back in a while."

She nodded and went back to reading the magazine.

Hal shrugged and sat down in Frank's ancient wooden office chair. It squeaked loudly in protest.

Frank headed for interview room two. He closed the door behind him as he entered and found a middle aged woman, probably on the high side of forty, with chestnut brown hair, that must've come out of a bottle given the lines on her face. She wore a pair of faded blue jeans, white Nike's, and powder blue shirt with a green and yellow scarf tied around her thin neck. She had a haughty expression on her tanned face as if this was wasting her time from being at the country club. Her lipstick was subdued shade of pale pink and her dark sunglasses sat perched atop her head.

Her legs were crossed and she looked uncomfortable in the steel unpadded chair. But then who needed comfort when you were being interrogated.

"Hello, Ms. Sommers…"

"That's Mrs. Sommers of the Hampton Sommers," she said with the roll of her pale blue eyes.

"Huh…sorry." He sat across from Mrs. Sommers and studied her. Expensive jewelry hung off her wrists, ears and fingers and her clothes were designer label so she was money and lots of it. Her perfume filled the room with its light fragrant jasmine.

As you'd expect not so much as to be overpowering.

"So, Mrs. Sommers you say you killed Mr. Butters. Now why might that be?"

She shifted her narrow posterior on the chair and winced. "He was going to give in — to his wife."

"How's that?" Frank eyed her.

"She wanted him to lower his standards and that wasn't right for a writer of his caliber." The way she said it indicated that this information should be obvious to him.

"Mrs. Butters said that the gift you sent him, and the note that accompanied it, led him to tell his wife that he'd never give in to her demands. She says that's why she killed him."

To his surprise Mrs. Sommers snorted before she said, her voice dripping with sarcasm, "That's what I'd expect her to say. No, I assure you, detective, I killed him, not that woman."

Frank shook his head in wonderment. This situation was crazy, unlike anything he'd encountered in twenty years on the police force. Two confessions to the same murder and both killers trying to convince him they'd committed the act. This didn't make sense.

They were interrupted by a knock on the door and Hal's head stuck through an opening in the door. "Frank?"

Russ Crossley

Frank glanced at the younger man and nodded. Hal closed the door softly.

Frank turned his attention back to Mrs. Sommers as he stood to leave. "I'll be right back."

"I'm not going anywhere," Mrs. Sommers said with a cool edge to her voice that would've made a penguin seek warmer climes.

Still shaking his head as if he were in a dream Frank left the room to join Hal in the hallway outside. The younger man was pacing now and the gum in his mouth was getting a complete work out.

"What is it — Hal?"

"The ME's report came back…"

"Well, don't keep me waiting what did it say?"

"Mr. Butters died from acute appendicitis. The digitalis he found in the remains would've been insufficient to kill him. He was already dead when the fire started."

Hal's face paled. "And, Peterson from the FD called. He said the room where the body was found was locked from the inside given the door knob found at the site. These two may be attempted killers but — he died of natural causes."

Frank's face dropped and became the shade of fine wood ash. He gazed at Hal his eyes wide. What would he tell these two old women?

They hadn't murdered Mr. Butters? Did he lay attempted murder charges or not? And what about the Captain? How would he react when the case that had been a slam dunk fell apart?

What a mess. He closed his eyes and his chin sank to his chest. He brought fingers to both temples and rubbed trying in vain to ease the growing headache.

Opening his eyes, Frank sighed. "You stay here, Hal, I'm gonna go see the captain." He turned away from his partner and started the long walk to the captains office.

He stopped outside the office door and gripped the doorknob. He rapped his knuckles of his free hand on the door. "Come, came the muffled reply.

Holding his breath he threw the door open and entered the door thudding closed after him. The captain sat behind his desk his attention on his computer screen. As Frank sat down in one of the two leatherette chairs on the opposite side of the desk, Captain Reilly shifted in his seat and faced Frank. Frank let out the breath he'd been holding.

"Uhhh, sir, there's been a development in the Butters case."

The captain sat in silence his brow wrinkled. "It seems it took more than two to kill Mr. Butters. Sir."

Frank cringed waiting for inevitable explosion. This was going to be a long complicated night, and the captain hated complicated.

About the Author

International selling author, Russ Crossley writes romance under the name R.G. Hart, mystery/suspense under the name R.G. Crossley, and science fiction and fantasy under his own. This year there will be re-issues the romantic comedies, Bachelorette: Zombie Edition by Champagne Books, and Antique Virgin by 53rd Street Publishing, paranormal romantic comedy, Zomopolis, and a new western romance entitled, The Fire In Their Hearts co-authored with R.S. Meger. In addition the near future suspense novel, The Last Serial Killer by R.G. Crossley was recently released by 53rd Street Publishing in ebook and trade paperback versions.

He has sold several short stories that have appeared in anthologies from Pocket Books, St. Matins Press, at Smashwords, Amazon, and other e-retail sites.

With his wife, romance author R.S. Meger, he owns and operates a small press publishing company, 53rd Street Publishing.

The company began in April 2011 and now has over one hundred e-book titles and a number of print titles, with more planned in 2012 and 2013.

He is a member of SF Canada and the Greater Vancouver Chapter of Romance Writers of America. He is also an alumni of the Oregon Coast Professional Fiction Writers Master Class taught by award winning author/editors, Kristine Katherine Rusch and Dean Wesley Smith.

To find a complete listing of his work check out his website http://www.rghart.com, http://russstory. blogspot.com.Razor's blog can be found at http:// razorandedge.blogspot.com

Feel free to contact him on Facebook or Twitter. He loves to hear from readers

Other books by the Author

Razor and Edge Mysteries
The Kidnapping of Billy Buttons
String of Pearls
Death by Clown
Beggin' For Murder
Ragged Ice
The Grand Central Mystery
A Strange Case of Undead Murder

Jazz Stiletto Mysteries
A Day Without Sunshine
Skullduggery
Instrument of justice (first published in Over My Dead
Body online mystery magazine)

The Amanda Dark paranormal mysteries
Hook Island
Grind Manor
Moonrise Diner

The Trudy Wilson Mysteries
Bad Loyalty
Shear Murder
Buzzcut coming in 2015

Novels
Attack of the Lushites
Revenge of the Lushites
My Zombie Prince

Antique Virgin
The Fire In Their Hearts
with R.S. Meger (from Champagne Books)
Zomopolis
The Last Serial Killer

Short Stories
Countdown
Shoeless Moe
Round Up At The Burger Bar:
The Story of Trixie Pug, Parts 1, 2, 3, 4, 5, 6, 7, 8, 9
Five Minutes
Blossom Queen, Barbarian
The Secret
The Family Line
End of the Flies
Death by Magic
The Penguin Sleeps With The Fishes
Only The Worthy
Hero For A Day
End of Empire
Strange Bedfellows
Big Business
A Perfect Crime
The Wise Guy and The Pirates
In Search of the Perfect Cup
T.I.N. Men
The Legend of G and the Dragonettes
The Incredible Mr. Fix-It
Lock Stock and Barrel
Divided Loyalties
Cave of Wonders

A Family Empire
Until We Meet Again
Dragon Rising
Solitary Man
The Keel Mountain Conspiracy
Angel on My Shoulder
Heroes of Old
The Great Bicycle Race
Tikka's Big Day
"My Partner the Zombie" —
Hungry For Your Love Anthology
(St. Martin's Press)
Big Hairy Deal
One Red Shoe
A Bad Day in Lunden Texas
Bloody Betty, Queen of the Pirates
Mirror Image
Dangerous Waters
Cape Disappointment
Boomerang
The Watcher of Wayburn Street
The Apprentice
Drip!
A Beautiful Friendship and The Parrot of Doom
Robine's Diary
The Christmas Club
Loose Ends
Splatter Pattern
It Takes Two
Lexicon

Anthologies
Tales of Urban Fantasy
Five Tales of Bizarre Detectives
Tales of Mystery and Suspense
Tales of Weird Fantasy
Spies, Detectives, & Heroes
Tales of Twisted Crime
Tales of The Unexpected
Tales From Space
10 by Russ Crossley
Round Up At The Burger Bar: The Story of Trixie Pug,
Parts 1- 5 The Beginning
Worlds of Science Fiction and Fantasy
More Tales of Mystery and Suspense
Ladies of the Jolly Roger
Justice Served
Love Stories
Ladies of the Jolly Roger with R.S. Meger
The Adventures of Razor and Edge:
Five Tales From The Quirky Detective Team

Non-Fiction
The Writers Tools - The Synopsis

Also available from 53rd Street Publishing.

In this exciting prequel to Bad Loyalty we first meet hairdresser, Trudy Wilson.

Trapped in a marriage to a drunk for a husband she faces a failing business and a dead woman, Sharon Carstairs, she's suspected of murdering

To clear herself and find the real murderer Trudy joins forces with Sharon's biker brother, Bruce. Join them on a terrifying ride to a highway of fear, murder and conspiracy to discover the terrible truth.

A truth they both fear.

This first book of the Trudy Wilson Mysteries is available now at your favorite ebook retailer or bookstore. The latest book in the series, Buzzcut, will be released in the fall of 2015.

www.ingramcontent.com/pod-product-compliance
Lightning Source LLC
Chambersburg PA
CBHW021059130626
46552CB00005B/2180